DON'T TELL A SOUL

JOSHUA RAVEN

Red
Ink.
Publishing

First published in the UK by Blue Fish Publishing Limited in 2007. This edition was published in the UK by Red Ink Publishing Limited, 2025.

© 2024 Red Ink Publishing Limited www.5fingers.co.uk

5fingers is a trademark of Red Ink Publishing Limited.

This novel is a work of fiction. Names and characters are the product of the author's imagination, and any resemblance to actual persons, living or dead, is entirely coincidental.

A catalogue record for this book is available from the British Library

Cover Design by JD Smith.

Title Production by The BookWhisperer

ISBN(eBook): 978-1-0685674-0-7
ISBN(Paperback): 978-1-0685674-1-4
ISBN(Hardcover): 978-1-0685674-2-1

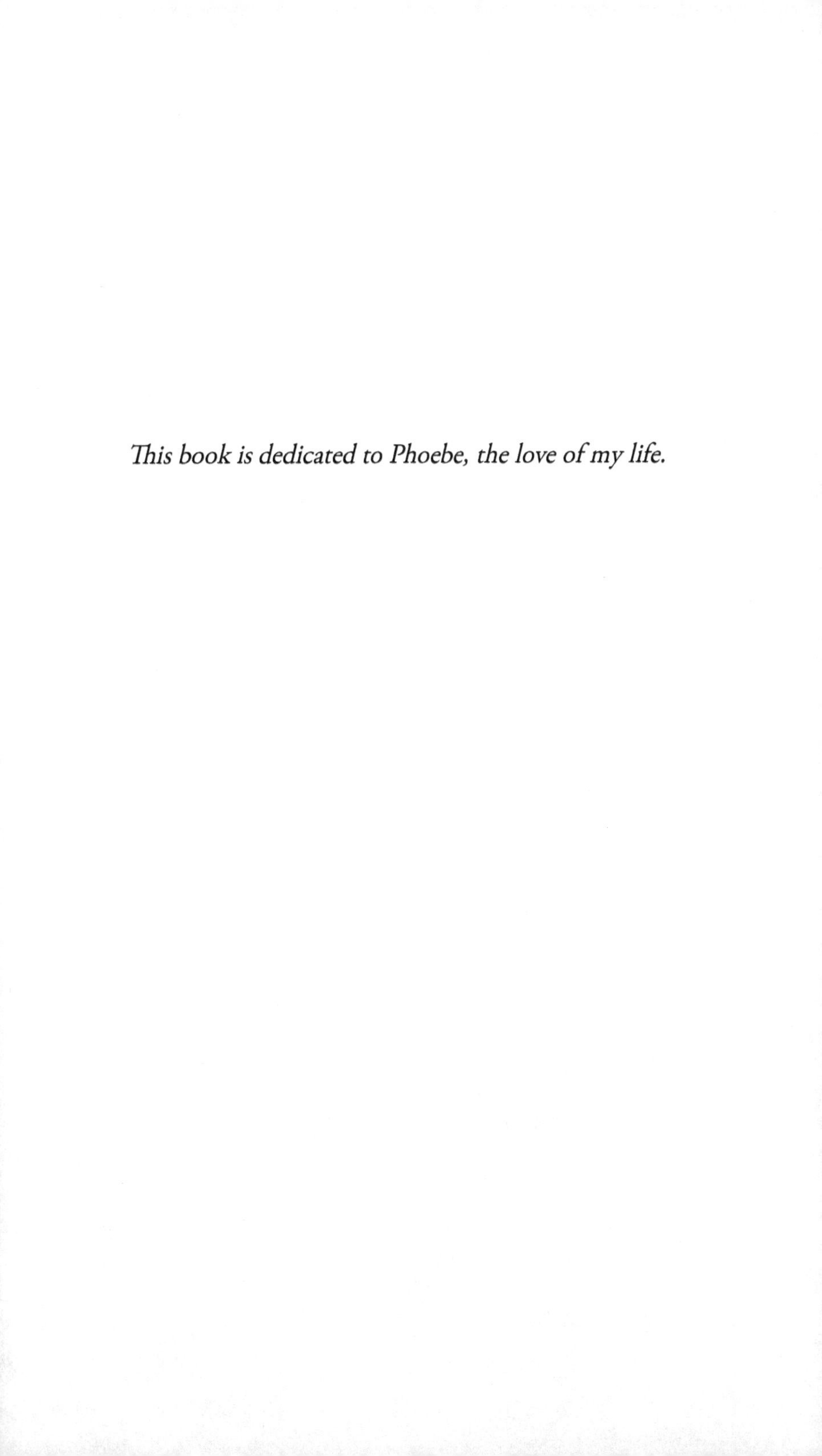

This book is dedicated to Phoebe, the love of my life.

One two three four five
Once I caught a fish alive

CHAPTER 1

It was midnight on the last day of term. The end of the world had come and gone, and Rachel Race had survived.

So many emotions hit her now everything that was familiar had come to an end. Even the things she hated or the things that bored her, like revision or double maths.

She lay in her bed, weightless, staring at the spectral moon. There were no clouds, just a black sky riddled with stars.

The glow from a distant streetlight touched the objects in her room. In the summertime, Rachel preferred to leave her curtains and window open so she could feel the breeze on her face. It had been some years since she had really been scared of the dark. It was, in fact, seven years because seven years ago, her mother lay dead, and Rachel's world had dissolved into darkness.

1₂₃₄₅

For Rachel, her mother, Maryam, was the most beautiful woman in the world. Maryam had indeed been beautiful. Born and raised in the lush green countryside of southern India, she had radiated sunshine throughout her life. Although Rachel had never visited her mother's hometown, its landscape was so familiar to her. The stories her mum had told her made it all so vivid. She felt like she knew every building and every hill that her mother knew.

As Rachel gazed at the night sky, she pictured her mum's big smiling eyes, eyes which Rachel had inherited. Not a day went by when she did not think of her mum. Does the pain ever go away? For her dad, the pain had never gone away. It was a long time since she had heard the story of how her parents had met. He never spoke of it now. He was a young, fresh-faced English teacher from Birmingham, England, working abroad. His work had taken him to southern India. There, the sun was lemon yellow and hot all the time, and the vibrant colours made you dizzy.

When he laid eyes on Rachel's mother, his heart raced.

But that was all a very long time ago, and Rachel no longer knew that man. She now shared a house with a stranger, a shadow of his old self, and she feared him.

RACHEL HAD LIVED her whole life in the seaside city of Griffton, in the south of England. In city terms, it was small. An escarpment overlooked the city from the north, which the locals fondly called Griffton Cliff. A long line of beach edged the southern part. Tall buildings rose from the centre, with the City Council buildings, Griffton College, the Cathedral, and various businesses forming the highest silhouettes. Circling these was row upon row of houses.

Rachel's house lay in a nondescript row of a nondescript suburb of Griffton. Number 42 Russet Road was tucked out of sight, somewhere on Griffton's east side.

Her father, Eddie, lay snoring softly on the sofa as the television winked and murmured. In her room, Rachel lay staring at the moon through big brown eyes, half closed. Around her face was a pool of wavy brown hair dyed blue at the tips.

Conversations from the day returned to her mind.

She was standing in the schoolyard with a group of school friends. "I can't believe it's over!" cried one.

"All those exams!" exclaimed another.

"I'm going to burn my coursework now," vowed Rachel. "No more maths ever again."

"And no more Mrs Goyle!"

But amidst the euphoria of the end of term, real life was starting to break in.

"What are we meant to do now? What are any of us going to do now? I mean, I can't go to college – I reckon I've failed everything. And I don't know if I'm ready to work. Not properly, anyway," moaned Rachel.

"Let's think about it tomorrow," said her best friend, Lara Summer, soothingly. "Tonight, we celebrate."

❧ 12345 ❧

LATER ON, they went to their local pub, the Pirate's Paradise, where kids were allowed in as long as they behaved themselves and stuck to soft drinks.

There, Rachel spoke to Lara, demanding, "What do you mean you're going away?"

"I know I should have told you, Rach. But dad didn't want anyone to know until it was all sorted. I'm sorry I didn't say. I really am. You see, dad got a big job offer, and he wants us all to go with him. Me, mum, and Joel. Out to California. It was the sort of offer he couldn't turn down."

"So, you're leaving me," sighed Rachel.

"I suppose I am," said Lara.

"When are you going?"

"Next month."

Rachel's eyes glazed over as she gazed into an empty future. Lara and Rachel had been best friends forever. This was not going to be easy.

12345

Back in bed, through sleepy eyelids, Rachel saw a cloud pass over the moon. The trees in the garden rustled. Then she started to have that dream again.

She dreamt of a long mountain range somewhere in the east.

Perhaps it was in India or Tibet. These were, however, not places she had been to. She had never actually left England, but these snowy mountains were so familiar. The angular rocks and massive, sheer drops, the white sky above, the deep chasms, and treacherous wind. There was no life to be seen, just one abyss after another.

Then she focused on one particular mountain. This one looked dangerous and impossible to climb. Death and darkness hung around it.

In the background, Rachel heard the mountain range rumbling.

She slipped further into an uneasy sleep.

12345

In the early hours, Rachel Race felt a stabbing pain in her left hand. Instinctively, she grabbed her left hand with her right. Doubling over with pain, she rolled out of bed and onto the floor. Her hand felt like it was burning. A searing pain tore at her fingers.

As she looked down under the glow of the streetlight, she saw the blood. There was so much blood. It covered everything.

It pulsed from the stump of her little finger, soaking her duvet. Where on earth was her little finger?

Helpless with pain, she clamped her right palm over the wound and screamed.

There was a flutter of wings at the open window.

CHAPTER 2

At first, the pain was unbearable. It was like fire and ice and acid all in one, setting her left hand alight. It was like no other injury she had ever experienced. Her brain was saturated with raw nerve activity.

But soon, something else kicked in that seemed to pull Rachel through the pain. It was a hard-nosed calmness. Where it came from was a mystery.

With eyes wide open and mouth squeezed shut, she hunted for her finger. She searched the folds of the bedclothes and rummaged around the floor, one-handed. She made sure the search was systematic, going from one end of the bed to the other and then on to the floor.

"This is what they always tell you," she told herself. "Find the finger and put it on ice. I just have to find it. I need to go downstairs. Look for a bag of frozen peas."

She had no idea where she had found this strange calmness. It certainly wasn't like her. Her friends would normally describe her as emotional and even irrational. "She cries a lot and is a bit unstable," they would say. Or perhaps, "She's a bit temperamental and prone to shouting." "She's always scared of something or other." And they were right.

But as she hunted methodically, she found herself growing calm. It was a pleasant sensation, completely new to her. It steadied her as she looked for the finger.

Then, as quickly as the calmness had come over her, it subsided. As she forced herself to stand up, cradling her maimed hand, a dark fear came over her. This was more like the Rachel she knew. Her mind spun out of control. *What if the attacker is still in the house? What if he is in the room? Could he be hiding by the wardrobe or outside the door? What if it was an animal on the loose? A lion or a tiger!*

She stared around her room. "Where is it? Is it going to jump out at me?" she panicked.

Nothing looked out of place, apart from the blood. Everything was as it was when she had turned in. Her guitar by the wardrobe, the pile of school course work in the corner, and the bangles and beads on the shelf.

She seemed to have stemmed the blood flow for now, through the pain, by applying as much force as she could muster.

But she was left with the stump of her little finger with two joints missing, and she just couldn't find the rest of it. It was a desperate situation.

The fear rose up again like the flow of blood from her finger. "I can't stay here," she said, surprised by the sound of her own voice.

Milky moonlight touched her pyjamas, which were wet with blood. Electric currents of pain fired up her left arm and reached down into her left leg. She found a scarf and bound up her hand as best she could.

Then she left the room.

HER FATHER WASN'T in his bedroom. His door was open, and his bed was unmade. As she went downstairs, she noticed he was no longer on the sofa where he had been. The TV was still flickering in the dark. The room smelled of cigarettes and drink, as usual.

She looked through into the kitchen. There was no sign of him there either.

She glanced again at the sofa. There was an impression where he had been sitting, but he was not in the room. She saw an empty whisky bottle lying on the floor nearby.

Nearby was another.

It hit her like a truck. There was, in reality, no one else in the house tonight when she lost her finger. No one was in but her and her dad. There really was only one person who could have hacked off her finger.

Things were bad between them and had been ever since Mum had died. In fact, they had got worse over the last few months. But this took it up to a whole new level.

She glanced again at the empty bottles. Her dad should not be drinking on anti-depressants, but there was no telling him.

She heard a bump upstairs and instinctively tilted her head towards the stairs. He didn't emerge, but she didn't want to wait around. She bolted for the front door, pushed her toes into her shoes, and grabbed a cardigan from the coat hook.

The air was cool on her cheeks. Russet Road was cloaked in shadows. All was silent except for the breeze through distant trees and the faraway hiss of the English Channel. Parked cars dotted the curbside, all dulled into tones of grey by the night sky.

Wincing again, Rachel pulled on her cardigan. Jolts of pain leapt through her body. The scarf reddened as the blood made its relentless way to the surface.

Lara lived on a road around the corner on Ruby Street. Sometimes, Rachel would escape there to take a break from her dad, particularly when he had been drinking.

Rachel set off on the familiar journey at a brisk walking pace. She pulled her mobile phone from her cardigan pocket and texted Lara with one hand. "In trouble, coming round," read the text. It wasn't the first time she had sent this message.

"She's going to be asleep," Rachel muttered. She pressed send anyway, and the phone chimed.

Before she had reached the end of her road, a voice arrested her, slurring her name.

She knew it was her father.

She was determined not to turn back but to keep heading for Lara's house. She set her jaw and marched on. Her friend's house was along this pavement, and then right, another fifty or sixty paces, down another road, through the children's park, and then a dogleg and a loop. She knew the route so well from years of popping back and forth.

She felt eyes on her back and made the mistake of looking around.

Over her shoulder, she saw the looming mass of her dad, illuminated by the streetlight on the main road. Unshaven, his face was troubled by shadows. He was in his dressing gown and had his slippers on.

He was carrying their long kitchen knife in his right hand. Rachel stifled a scream.

*1*2345

Running now, Rachel reached the end of the road in half a dozen strides. She passed the black taxi – that was first base. Second base was the post box, and she made it to this by sprinting with her head down. She patted the base with the palm of her right hand as she passed it. Third base would be the park.

Her mind raced as she tried to fight off the fear. Past events resurfaced in her memory.

It was Christmas Eve. They had been without her mum for four years, and Rachel was thirteen. Dad had been drinking all day. She had been out playing at Lara's. By the time she had wandered back home, he was in a fine state.

It started as a lecture but became a rant as the afternoon wore on. By the end of the evening, tears streaming down her face, she got to see her presents. He tore them open one by one, smashed them up, and then attacked the tree. All the care that he had put in to make it an 'extra special' Christmas evaporated by the second.

Rachel spent the rest of Christmas at Lara's. Of course, he apologised afterwards and even bought her extra presents. But the damage was done.

She had made it to third base, the park. It was a small, square children's play area where the mums met to chat during the day. At night, it was deserted and still.

As she raced across the middle of the tarmac, up to the slide, the roundabout, and the little line of swings, her bandage started to unravel. Steeped in thick blood, it began to ooze again. Rachel gasped and bundled her hand under her right armpit. Although this secured it for now, it hindered her running.

Suddenly, Eddie appeared at the side entrance to the square park, beyond the railings.

He was too far to grab her but close enough to outpace her if he used the full length of his strides. He was a tall man, over six feet, compared with Rachel, who was five-two. Rachel cast him a sidelong glance and reached the central slide. He approached the park gate, knife in hand.

Rachel's eyes widened.

LARA WAS sound asleep in bed. Somewhere in a dream, she heard the polyphonic tone that told her that Rachel was sending her a text message.

Lara had enjoyed the last day of term immensely, particularly the bit where they all went out to the Pirate's Paradise to celebrate.

The Paradise was a cosy pub down on the beach which

allowed young people to enter without having to show any identification. They were not allowed to buy alcohol, though. The rule was they had to keep their noses clean, stick to soft drinks, and keep the noise down. Most of their gang were around sixteen, though some were still only fifteen, and it was a wonder that Alan, the owner, managed to keep his licence.

They sat in a booth around a wooden table marked with rings of dark beer from an earlier group of drinkers. Lara was a big fan of ginger ales and had drunk a good number tonight and laughed a lot. Rachel, on the other hand, had been morose and irritable, even before she had told her about the move.

She was fond of Rachel but was looking forward to the new adventures ahead. Her father was moving the family to California in a month. She liked Californian boys, particularly the ones she had seen in the films. One of her favourite bands, Red Hot Chili Peppers, was also from California, where loads of famous people lived. It also had great weather and better TV.

She imagined there were also some fancy bars in California, not that she disliked the Paradise. The noise from the fruit machines could be a bit too much, and the boys could get a bit irritating by the end of the evening. But that said, the Paradise had become part of who she was.

Anyway, when she'd told Rachel about moving to America, it was like Rachel's world had ended. You'd think Rachel would be excited about her moving to the States. Instead, Rachel just kept going on about stuff they'd done over the years. It was almost like she was the one who was going away.

Although she loved Rachel and they had been friends for years, they weren't joined at the hip. Sometimes, Rachel acted like they were. Lara really wanted to have her own adventures and her own life. Was she selfish thinking like that?

She knew all the bad stuff that had happened in Rachel's life, with her mother and all. There was that time when her dad went away for a week without telling anyone. He left Rachel in the house with a stack of ready meals and little else. This was a few years ago. It was good that no one found out about it because Rachel was still a kid then.

But worse, he was always shouting at her about the smallest thing. Lara couldn't live like that. She didn't know what she would do if her dad was like that. She was just glad he wasn't. Also, she wasn't a hundred percent sure about it, but did Rachel's dad hit her as well? Rachel would never tell her about that, not ever. On some occasions, when Rachel came over to escape, she suspected things had gotten out of hand, and Rachel looked a bit battered. But she always remained silent when quizzed.

So, somewhere along the way, their lives got intertwined. "Call Lara and Rachel," people always said. "Where's Lara and Rachel? Lara and Rachel are coming…" It was as if they were one person with two names. They were best friends: inseparable. They hung out together, broke the rules together, and talked incessantly. "But all good things come to an end," thought Lara, "and now is a good time to break free and see what I'm missing."

When Lara's head hit the pillow, the end of the term swiftly receded, along with the teachers, the friends, the Pirate's Paradise, and Rachel's strange mood. Black slumber cascaded over her like dry ice tumbling from the stage of a Red Hot Chili Peppers gig. Lara slept.

12345

RACHEL'S DAD stopped at the park gate. Unfit and panting, he stooped over and put his hands on his hips. His ragged breathing left him unable to speak. Absent-mindedly, he held the long blade at his side.

Rachel took the opportunity to bolt out of the other exit across the central square. The chase was on.

She had made it to third base: the park. Home base was Lara's house, which was along a dogleg and round a loop.

She moved past more dark houses with their curtains drawn, but her pace was slower now. She felt sleepy. Her hand was bleeding more now. Strawberry-jam blood seeped through the material bandage and glistened on the surface.

She knew her dad was behind her, jogging along the pavement as she trotted towards Lara's house, but she was still faster than him.

HER HEAD FELT light as she reached Lara's door and knocked quietly with her right hand. Lara's house rose up three storeys high, a sheer cliff face made of brick. There was no answer from within. The curtains were drawn. Rachel was feeling cold now: very cold. Her arms tingled.

She knocked again and rang the bell. Behind her, she heard her father approach, his heavy steps catching up with her at last.

As Rachel smiled and then collapsed, he caught her in his arms, dropping the knife on Lara's drive.

CHAPTER 3

Rachel blinked away her dream. A white ceiling came into view, lit by a long tube light. There was a smell of antiseptic in the air. She interrogated her brain to work out where on earth she was.

In her dream, mice had been gnawing at her hand. They had been chewing on a finger: her little finger. The sensation returned to her left hand. She felt a dull throb there.

"I'm in hospital," she murmured to herself. A female voice nearby told her to relax and try not to talk for now. She closed her eyes.

Flashbulb memories came back to her. *A face in the mirror. The young Rachel Race, aged nine. Huge brown eyes. A long fringe over her face. There is horror in her eyes at losing her mother.*

Another flashbulb memory invaded. *Her and Lara are paddling in the sea. A winter sky behind them. The sea is ice cold. Lara laughs.*

Then, another memory came. *The children's park. A cat has cut its paw on some broken glass in the alley nearby. Tiny droplets of blood redden the green rubberised tarmac. She is sad.*

Then she had a memory of the mountains. But she had

never been to any mountains that were this big. *A bleak landscape made up of tall, spiky peaks covered in snow. Perhaps it is from a magazine picture or a programme she has seen. The mountains rumble, emitting a strange and low aircraft sound.*

Rachel stirred uneasily in her hospital bed.

The next set of memories was longer. *Her mother bathed in light. It is summer. A birthday picnic. Green grass and hills and a deep blue sky. It's a strange combination of colours when you think about it, green hills and bright blue sky, but that's nature. They'd been up on Griffton Cliff, the huge steep escarpment to the north which overlooks the city and the sea.*

Her mother is singing a song she made up for Rachel in English and Malayalam. The English verses are slow and ponderous, but the verses in her native tongue speed up and slow down, having a rhythm of their own. Her dad is lying on a rug. He grins from under a wide-brimmed sun hat. Hot sun washes over them. She is happy.

Another memory. She is visiting her father's family in Solihull, the newer part of Birmingham. His large family of 'Silhillians' has just taken the young Rachel out to Malvern Park. This is a massive park linked to another massive one called Brueton Park, near the town centre, and it covers 130 acres. Rachel would tell her friends all this when she got back home.

She plays on the swings and sees the athletic track, the swimming pool, and the mini-golf course. There is a little stream where children are fishing. Someone has caught a stickleback with three sharp points in its back. It is fantastic, and she is thrilled.

They walk for miles. Back at Grandpa's eight-bedroom detached house, Grandpa tells a few funny stories and falls asleep in a chair. Grandma drinks tea with mum and Auntie Dorothy. Rachel and her cousins, Ben, Dave, and Lucy, go off to play hide and seek. The house is a perfect place for a small girl like her to hide. But then she falls asleep in a wardrobe, and they haven't found her for ages. She is scared.

1⁄2345

"DID ANYONE FIND MY FINGER?" Rachel asked one of the nurses who was attending to her. She was a plump woman with kind eyes. She wore a badge with a happy, smiling face on it. Above the yellow face was a name badge saying Martha Grace. Rachel's gaze drifted to the pale blue wall behind the nurse. This was the second coherent sentence Rachel had uttered since she'd passed out outside Lara's house. The first had been, "I'm in hospital," some hours previously.

The nurse smiled and said, "The doctor will be here soon, and he will tell you all he can."

She lifted her upside-down watch, which was pinned to her uniform, and peered at it. Then she wrote something down.

"Am I going to be all right?" asked Rachel. Then she added, "Is my dad here?"

"You just rest, and the doctor will be along to see you. You're going to be just fine."

1⁄2345

THE DAY CONTINUED in this vein—flashbulb memories mixed with flashbulb meetings.

Rachel was in the children's ward at Griffton General Hospital. They called it Citron Ward, and her sheets did smell vaguely lemony. Next to Rachel's bed was a metal trolley for her things. She didn't have many things to put on it, she thought. There was only her cardigan, folded up and placed on a shelf with her mobile phone on top of it. Someone had put out a couple of teen novels for her on the top and a Disney clock. It said 11:49.

She also had her own open curtain, which stopped a few inches from the ground. It had flowers and butterflies on it.

There were a dozen other beds in her ward. No one was up to chatting, and most seemed to doze the day away. For example, one girl was asleep in the far corner, near the window. Another girl in a bed three down had her leg in plaster, raised up on a pulley. Rachel could see her chest rise and fall as she slept.

The pain in her fingers had gone. Her left hand itself was wrapped in a thick bandage, like a valuable item ready for posting.

Soon, the doctor came. He introduced himself as the consultant who had carried out some surgery on her. They had decided to anesthetise her completely for the procedure, and it all went well.

He outlined "the procedure" as far as he could without making Rachel feel queasy. Apparently, they had tied, stitched, bound, and dressed this and that and seemed happy with the work. It had taken some specialist nerve work, and that was why they had knocked her out. She learned that some very long nerves ended in the fingers, and so did some heavy-duty arteries. It wasn't simple stuff they were doing here; far from it.

"Did anyone find my finger?" she asked.

Sadly, no, lamented the doctor. He made some conciliatory noises anyway. But Rachel knew they were just words.

Her eyes welled up.

"Is there anything you need?" he asked her. Well, she had a load of questions. For starters, where was her finger? Next, who took it? Then there was the question of her father. What was he up to, chasing her with a knife like that? Where was he now? Where was Lara when she needed her? Why did her mother have to die? Why was life so senseless and meaningless? Why her, anyway?

But instead, she just said, "I'm a bit hungry. Any chance of some food?"

THE POLICE ROLLED in after lunch. Rachel had eaten a rather lacklustre lasagne that was low on taste but high on substance. It made her feel ill. She wasn't used to eating anything more than a few lettuce leaves. But she felt ravenous, so the fantastic plastic lasagne had to suffice.

The tall officer addressed her as Miss Race and came to her bare-headed, cap in hand. She had a deep voice and was accompanied by a smaller officer with a kind face and a twinkle in her eye. They were Officer Hardwick and Officer Bloom.

Rachel was sitting up in her bed now. Nurse Martha fussed around her.

"I'm afraid we have some bad news about your father, Miss Race," blurted Officer Hardwick.

"Rachel," she mumbled instinctively.

"This may be difficult to hear right now, Rachel, but we had to take your father into custody," barked the officer officiously.

Rachel must have looked shocked.

"I know this will be hard for you," murmured Officer Bloom. "But if you're up to talking…"

"We need to take a statement from you if you're ready," barked Officer Hardwick. "Just to ascertain the events of last night as you remember them."

Rachel nodded.

"Just take your time," she snapped.

Rachel told them about the evening, leaving out the bit about going to the Pirate's Paradise pub because she didn't want to get them or her friends into trouble. Besides, it wasn't as though she was drinking alcohol or anything. Then she told them about waking up in the night with a sharp pain in her hand. Next, she talked about how she hunted for the finger. Then she told the story of how she ran from the house with her father chasing after her. She purposefully didn't tell them about the knife.

"You should be aware that after your father brought you into the hospital, we found a kitchen knife in a rosebush outside the house in Ruby Street."

Rachel raised both eyebrows.

"It had your father's fingerprints on it," growled Officer Hardwick.

"You don't think he…" shuddered Rachel.

"We found very high levels of alcohol in your father's blood, Rachel. We intend to hold him in custody for the time being, for your own safety," the Officer barked.

"We're not drawing any conclusions just yet, Rachel," said Officer Bloom, as kindly as she was able.

Rachel slumped back in her bed and closed her eyes.

"We are interested in what's best for you," Nurse Martha Grace said. "Someone will come to visit you soon, just to see how things are going."

"I'm fine," sulked Rachel. She wondered why Lara hadn't been to see her or even sent back a text.

"It won't hurt to chat things through," soothed the nurse.

Rachel stared out of the long windows opposite. Out on a flat rooftop, a nurse sat in a chair and had her break. She had her face turned towards the sun.

"Good for her," she thought.

Late afternoon, Iona, her friend from work, came to see her.

Rachel liked Iona. Iona had braided hair and a rainbow dress with customised Dr Martens boots. She was twenty, four years older than Rachel, and she spoke in a breathy, girly-swirly voice. Rachel had been to Iona's flat once, and it was full of coloured glass ornaments and bright furry rugs. The place had a sweet aroma of tangerines.

They worked together on Saturdays at Rock and Shock, a local record shop overlooking the beach. Today was Saturday.

"I came as soon as I could. Your text was so weird. I mean, I was trying to work out what you meant by 'in hospital.' Like, were you trying to say you were visiting someone, or that you were really sick, or what? I told Ben, like you asked. He seemed cool about it. He said it had to be serious because you've never missed a day of work. Not like me. I mean, Rock and Shock is fun, but I need my duvet days! So, tell me, what happened to your hand?"

"Oh, I had an accident."

"With a chainsaw? They've wrapped it up pretty big, with all that stuff on it, you know."

"I don't really want to talk about it."

"Oh, okay." Iona folded her arms as if to say, 'Suit yourself, then.' She grinned like a maniac and nodded at Rachel, making her braided hair jangle.

Rock and Shock was a fun place to work because Rachel loved music. It was also near the beach, which meant they could watch the sea and wander out on their breaks. Also, a lot of interesting people always drifted in. They ranged from skaters and surfers to holidaymakers from out of town.

There was rarely a dull day. She could line up the CDs and listen to all the new stuff she didn't have the money to buy. But she wasn't sure if she could work there full-time like Iona. It would drive her crazy.

It was left to Rachel to break the awkward pause. "Sorry. I mean, it's really nice you came to see me, Iona. How was work today?" asked Rachel.

Iona sparked into life again. "You know that guy who keeps coming in – I think he likes me – well, he bought another copy of the Golden Groove album. He just hung around the desk, and I'm like, 'Is there anything else?' and he just didn't want to leave!"

"It's so obvious," drawled Rachel. "Isn't it just?"

"Yeah – he loves our music selection so much that he just has to keep coming back for more."

"Don't tease, Rachel. He has got this cute little smile. So anyway," said Iona.

"Anyway," grinned Rachel.

"Some of us are going out tonight to the Crab. I suppose you're not up to it just yet?"

"Probably not," said Rachel.

"That's a shame. Oh well, Ben said rest up. I forgot to say," added Iona.

"Thanks for coming, Iona."

They exchanged goodbyes, and Iona jangled out of the ward, leaving Rachel thinking about just what she was going to do tonight – or any night from now on. She didn't fancy going back home after what had happened. It was too much to bear.

Also, she didn't think she could stay with Lara. If Lara was going away in a month, her parents would be packing up the house from now on. A sense of weariness washed over Rachel. Here she was, trapped in a hospital bed with nowhere to go, nothing to do, and no future. The pale blue walls held her in. The relentless tube light beat down on her. Her dad was in a local police station, probably hung over and hurting, and where was her so-called best friend?

*1*2345

RACHEL THOUGHT the social worker's visit had been fairly uneventful. They had talked about various things, and she had answered as best she could. Apparently, they were carrying out an initial assessment to find out what things were like at home. But for Rachel, it was just boring because it was something she didn't want to face. She wished they'd all just mind their own business.

The social worker, Hilary, had ascertained that Rachel Race lived with her dad, Eddie, and her mother, Maryam, had died seven years ago when Rachel was nine years old. There were no brothers or sisters. Hilary had also determined that most of

Rachel's family lived either in Solihull or Kerala, India, with little in between.

She had found out her dad had a tendency to drink heavily, as last night proved. Was he verbally abusive? Well, he was sometimes, but not all the time. But so was she. Was he physically abusive or threatening? No, not really, said Rachel, hugging her knees on the bed. She knew Hilary was watching her body language because she wasn't stupid. The truth was this whole exercise was making her feel self-conscious.

The question hung in the air: was he physically abusive or threatening? Well, there were the odd occasions when he took out his anger on objects around the house, she admitted. How did Rachel feel about these times, and what did she wish was the case? Well, it wasn't like she hadn't thrown a plate or two herself. Rachel laughed. She wasn't sure what Hilary thought of this. Was it the wrong thing to say?

Rachel talked things out, as the nurse had suggested, but it didn't particularly help her. She knew that in the end, Hilary was trying to work out whether she needed to be taken away from her father.

The bottom line was: did she think her dad had hacked off her finger? Did he then chase her with a kitchen knife to finish her off? Hilary hadn't specifically asked this, though they had danced around the questions. Rachel had been pondering this one all day. Was her dad a psycho?

"He can't be," she thought.

SHEEPISHLY, Lara crept in towards dinner time. Lara was pale and slim with shoulder-length black hair. She was the same height as Rachel and often wore black lipstick with black nail varnish.

"Look what the cat dragged in," breathed Rachel quietly. Then, she instantly regretted saying it.

"Well, I'm here, aren't I?" spat Lara. She scowled.

In reality, Rachel was exhausted now. She wasn't in the mood for a fight. She held her good hand out to Lara, making it into a fist. Lara made a fist, and they did their special handshake. It involved flexing their wrists and bashing their knuckles.

Lara's eyes were full of concern. "I did get your text eventually. You know I sleep in on a Saturday, and it's not like you haven't sent me that text before. The one about being in trouble."

"Great. Didn't you get my other texts?" queried Rachel.

"Course I did. I had things to do."

"What's more important than visiting me in hospital?"

"Like I said, I'm here, aren't I? So, what happened to you?"

"You mean you don't know? Didn't you, like, see the police at your house going through your front garden? They went, like, totally over the top," gaped Rachel.

"What are you going on about? I've been out all day," Lara snapped.

"You might as well grab a seat. I've got a few things I need to tell you," sighed Rachel, laying her head back on her pillow.

❧ 12345 ❧

TOWARDS THE END of visiting hours, Lake Emerson sauntered into the ward. Rachel's eyes widened.

Lake Emerson was a guy she knew who worked on the local paper. He had been to the shop a few times and was good friends with Lara's older brother, Joel. He was eighteen and a junior researcher at the Griffton News. Rachel got to know him after she had done a week of work experience there. She had also noticed he had hazel brown eyes and short treacle-coloured hair.

As he wandered in, he smiled to himself, spreading his wide jaw. He carried a small posy of flowers.

Rachel watched him wander over to the bed near the window, where the girl was asleep again. Her heart sank.

At the last minute, he turned around and grinned, bringing her the flowers and bowing.

"Actually, these are for you, Rachel," he mumbled, smiling. "Lake! Hi! But how did you know I was in here?" asked Rachel. "I was round at Joel's, and Lara was reading your text messages about your accident. Joel thought you could do with some cheering up!" he stuttered.

"Joel thought?"

"And I agreed." He hastily offered her the flowers.

Rachel was stunned into silence, but smiled sweetly, and nervously accepted the gift. She peeked out from behind her wavy brown hair, with its blue tips. "I don't know what to say," she sang out after a while. She had no idea he liked her, too.

The thought thrilled her.

"You don't have to say anything. Hey, want to hear some doctor jokes? A patient goes to his doctor and says, 'Doctor, I think I need glasses.' He gets told, 'You certainly do. This is a bank!'"

Rachel smiled.

"Or how about: 'Doctor, Doctor, I broke my arm in two places!' The doctor says, 'Well, stay out of those places then!'"

Rachel rolled her eyes.

"Okay, not so good. The patient says, 'My hair keeps falling out. What can you give me to keep it in?' The doctor says, 'How about a shoebox?'"

Rachel grinned.

"Try this: patient says, 'Doctor, I have a serious memory problem. I can't remember anything!' The doctor says, 'So, how long have you had this problem?' 'What problem?' says the patient!"

"Okay, stop. Have you, like, swallowed a joke book or something? I am feeling better now, but you have to promise to stop," laughed Rachel.

"It's a deal." Lake whipped out a pen and wrote something

down. "My number – in case you, er, need cheering up again," stammered Lake, losing his composure momentarily.

"I've got to run," he added and then made himself scarce. Rachel stared at the space where he had been standing.

1₂₃₄₅

IT WAS LATE EVENING, and the buildings outside Griffton General had greyed as the light faded. Rachel was on the second floor.

The ward was quiet now, and the lights were low. The night shift had come in and were out of sight. They'd done their final rounds and checks. Rachel yawned and slid her legs over the side of the bed. She felt the need to go for a walk.

She noted that the area was long and cool as she crossed it barefoot. Rachel was still wearing her pyjamas from the previous night. They had patches of dried blood down the sides. Her hand was heavy and uncomfortable as she moved.

She passed the nurses' desk, which was unoccupied. There was a flat-screen computer, a phone, several pens, and a large jug of water. The night staff must be hiding away in a back room. Not that there was much to do tonight.

Rachel found the bathroom and washed her face with her right hand. As she looked in the mirror, she noted the tiredness in her eyes.

It had been a very long twenty-four hours.

1₂₃₄₅

RACHEL RETURNED TO BED, pausing to look out of the hospital window. It was another clear black night with a smattering of white stars. Outside the windows, Griffton slept. She was on the side of the city, which had a view up to Griffton Cliff.

Griffton Cliff, which wasn't a real cliff, was a towering green and grey wall of stone and grass that overlooked the city. The escarpment dated back several centuries and had its roots in Griffton's quarrying industry. Rachel could glimpse the cliff between the buildings, but it mostly lay in darkness.

As she unfocused her eyes, she saw her reflection in the window. She saw a small girl with big brown eyes and waves of hair nursing a busted hand. She moved away.

Just then, the window exploded inwards, showering her legs with glass. She briefly glimpsed the teeth of the huge black panther as it flew towards her.

CHAPTER 4

Rachel scrambled backwards. She managed to get her body out of the panther's flight path. The black cat landed in the ward on the pads of his feet. He paused as Rachel continued to scramble backwards towards her bed.

She stared at the animal. He was huge. She had no chance against such a beast. If he decided to pounce again, that was the end.

Then, a wild thought occurred to her. *Did this panther take my finger last night? Is he back for more?* It was possible.

Just as Rachel seemed to reach the height of her fear, and her mind buzzed with thoughts of her own death, the panther drew away. Rachel stood shaking, desperately trying to think straight. Awash with panic.

Then, a sudden calmness descended on her. Just like last night. It was almost like someone else was in her body and was taking control. She breathed deeply and paused, watching the cat padding away slowly.

Thinking quickly, she grabbed her cardigan and phone. She could use the cardigan as a matador's cape to divert the panther if she needed to. What a wild thought! Then there was her phone. She'd need it to call for help if someone didn't come soon. She didn't recall ever having this much common sense, but then, she had never been in a situation like this before.

Rachel stood statue-still as the panther paced around the room, moving further away from her. He went to the furthest bed, where the girl by the window was still asleep. Rachel thought the glass shattering should really have jolted her out of her slumber. The girl with the broken leg was also asleep. The others also dreamed, unaware. It was so strange. Rachel winced as she imagined the cat taking a bite out of one of the sleeping girls. The thought was too horrible to entertain.

She watched the cat's muscles ripple under black fur as he pawed the cold floor. He had long whiskers and yellow eyes. Every so often, he bared his white fangs. His long white claws were out.

Rachel's pyjama trousers had protected her legs from the flying glass, but she still had to tread carefully. Glass had scattered far and wide across the floor.

Then she seized her opportunity and ran.

She left her bed behind her as she headed towards the nurses' station across the long room. The panther looked up quickly and decided to give chase. Rachel knew there was no way she could outrun him. It would be a battle of wits.

At the desk, there was still no one to be seen. Rachel slowed down and threw out her hand to catch the large jug of water. Swinging it in an arc, she splashed the water behind her as she ran. Water hit the floor like a wave and sent the panther skidding like a skittle toward a wall. He slammed into the wall at speed, hitting it with a thud.

Then she turned and threw the glass jug at the beast's head but missed by several inches. It smashed against the wall and rained down large chunks of glass over him. The panther shook his head. Angry now, he showed her his fangs and glowered.

Rachel gasped and ran as the cat hurtled after her again.

They raced down a long corridor. Rachel turned right into a

store cupboard. With seconds to spare, she turned and closed the door behind her.

It was dark inside. But this didn't matter for Rachel, who just wanted to get away from her pursuer.

Panting, she leaned back against the door. She waited in the darkened storeroom.

This was definitely one of the strangest things that had ever happened to her. She nursed her bandaged hand, folding her right forearm around it. Maybe it was the second strangest thing. The first strangest thing was losing her finger the night before.

Rachel raised her mobile phone to her face and looked at the illuminated screen. The phone told her there was no signal.

A SLOW MOANING came from the group of hooded figures. They were standing on Griffton Cliff in the darkness. In the distance, the sea hissed. The six figures wore long black cloaks. One had silver symbols and shapes embroidered on his. This figure was shorter than the rest. But his voice was lower than the rest. His moaning hit the lowest notes of the lot.

Tiny lights twinkled in the night sky. Stars, galaxies, nebulae, and aircraft all shone their lights. All the while, a cold breeze rippled over the cliff. It ruffled the dark garments of the hooded figures. A mist was descending on them as they moaned.

Before long, the mist had settled on them. It reached several feet above their heads and stretched out on either side of them.

The chanting started up again.

It was a shuddering, juddering sound, both guttural and monosyllabic.

The figures chanted out of tune, three low voices and three higher-pitched ones. The chanting seemed random at first. But it soon took on a rhythm of its own.

"*Sor-cah-yah. Hom-kii-ta-ray. Who-par-key. Yor-way-mah.*"

Inside the misty cloud that had settled on them, tiny lights sparkled.

They were standing near an old oak tree near the edge of the cliff. Its ancient arms were held aloft to embrace them. The city lay in the valley beneath Griffton Cliff.

The smaller hooded figure raised his arms. The chanting grew louder.

"*Son-kii-mah. Sor-cah-yah. Bah-loo-fey.*" Then silence.

The figures stood in the strange cloud, shrouded in a darkness that was darker than the night sky. The lights continued to twinkle inside it.

The figures were transfixed by the beauty of the lights. The smaller figure grinned under his hood and stared with bloodshot eyes.

"If she dies, she dies," he growled in a deep voice. "If not, well…" he added, grinning like a corpse.

"Samyaza will prevail," he stated.

"Samyaza will prevail," the others echoed.

All the while, the wind blew through his cloak, making the silver symbols glimmer as they reflected the lights.

12345

SOMETHING thudded into the storeroom door. Rachel recoiled. It must be the panther. He must have a very hard head.

She scrambled away from the door. But she found herself in a darker part of the room. The only source of light came from her mobile phone. It sent a haze into the storeroom. Holding her mobile phone out to shed more light around her, she saw shelves. On them were bandages, syringes, and swabs. The room was cold. She put on the cardigan and moved towards the far side of the room. There was another thud on the door. What was that panther trying to do? There was no way he was going to impact that door. It opened outwards.

She scanned the shelves, growing desperate.

She listened hard. No sound, and no one about. No night workers or nurses. Nor any patients, as far as she could hear. There was no sound except for the quiet hum of the tube lights and the sniffling and padding of the panther out in the corridor. She was trapped.

"THIS IS NOT HAPPENING," gasped Rachel. She had her back pressed hard against the door. There was another thud on the door. Rachel sunk down and leaned back against it. She did not know what else to do. She sat and waited. "Soon, he's going to lose interest," she said to herself. "He's bound to, isn't he?"

Some time passed. The little girl inside her cowered, and Rachel started to sniffle, her eyes welling up. It was at moments like these that she missed her mum the most.

The cat had been quiet for many minutes now. Wild-eyed, Rachel looked around her, holding her mobile phone out at arm's length. It radiated a weird glow, but it was just enough to see what was on the shelves. She spied some strange-looking glass bottles on a high shelf with liquid inside them. She tiptoed barefoot to the shelf and, standing on the balls of her feet, grabbed a handful of them.

In her mind, a plan was forming.

Thinking quickly, she turned and stepped lightly back to the storeroom door. She took a deep breath and listened hard. No sound. Gritting her teeth, she fought back her fear. Then she wiped her eyes, composed herself, and shouldered the door open.

She looked outside. There was no one there.

There was just a long, empty corridor that led back past the main desk and down to her ward. She stepped out with one foot while keeping the door open. Then she gathered her strength and threw the glass bottles as far down the corridor as possible.

She felt a ripple of pain, gnawing through her painkillers as she cast the bottles away.

The bottles smashed and spilled their contents onto the floor. Then Rachel heard the dreaded padding of heavy panther footsteps.

She peeked out from behind the door and waited.

Soon, the panther appeared around a left-hand corner. The cat made a noise that was a cross between a hiss and a roar. His teeth were visible. His eyes were red. He looked hungry. He trotted along the corridor, his nose and tail bobbing, to investigate the disturbance.

Rachel sneaked around the corner, hoping for an exit. Leaving the panther behind, she saw a long corridor ending in a double lift. It looked as though it was used for ferrying hospital beds between floors.

The corridor was lined with windows. They looked out onto the dark streets below. She looked at the lifts again.

She made light work of the corridor as she raced to the end and hit the button. Down below, she heard a lurching mechanical sound. The great pulley heaved the massive metal box up, but the lumbering machinery was too slow.

The big cat had appeared behind her at the end of the corridor, alerted by the noise. Rachel saw him pull back his muscular shoulders as he prepared to bound along the length of the corridor. She gasped, her mind reeling.

There was no time to wait for the lift.

RACHEL SPOTTED the staircase on the far left of the lift. She was on the second floor, which meant she had to descend two flights of stairs to get to the street level.

In seconds, she was through the door that led to the stairs. She had to push hard to open it. She was aware it closed slowly, in its own time. There was no time to force it. She took the stairs two at a time.

She made it down the first flight of a dozen stairs, ending in a square platform. Pictures of nurses and doctors-smiled down at her but couldn't help her now.

Wheeling round to the left, she hit another dozen steps. She landed on another square platform. She was on floor one. Does she exit here? No, that would narrow her options. There was nowhere to run.

She spun around the banister and faced another dozen steps, running down two or three at a time.

She heard a growl at the door above. He was here.

Rachel gasped and reached the square platform. Leaping down another twelve steps, she reached the ground floor where the exit was.

She was relieved to make it to the staircase door, but she was less relieved when it wouldn't pull open. She tried again. It wasn't budging. She pushed it this time, leaning her right shoulder into the panel, but still nothing. Why was it locked? It shouldn't be locked! *This is a public building,* she thought. Desperation started to wash over her.

The cat was descending the stairs above her. She could hear his footsteps. There was no way past him and no way out of the stairwell.

She took one desperate look at her mobile phone. There was still no signal.

She turned and saw another flight of stairs going down into the basement.

Her heart sank.

WITH NO OPTION but to go down further, Rachel turned and jumped down the remaining steps to the hospital's basement.

She quickly made it to the square platform, and several heart-beats later, she was at the basement door.

At the bottom, she turned back. That was when she saw the muscular panther stepping down onto the square platform she had just left. She had her back to the door and was trapped in the confines of the stairwell. She reached back behind her, scrabbling for the door handle. She turned it behind her back but also found it locked.

Between her and the predator was a solitary flight of stairs. The black panther rocked back onto his haunches. He licked his lips and geared up for the kill.

He didn't take his eyes off her as he sprang.

CHAPTER 5

Caleb Noble was his name.

The man, perhaps in his mid-forties, had sun-worn and weathered skin. He sat on the ground with his eyes closed behind his round black sunglasses. His legs were crossed in front of him, and his arms were in his lap. His head was bowed towards the earth, showing closely cropped grey hair. He sat perfectly still, concentrating.

Behind him, an impressive mountain range soared up and brushed the sky.

THE PANTHER HUNG in the air mid-flight. He looked like he was suspended on a steel cable. Rachel's mind boggled. His jaws were open, about to clamp onto her head, and his beady eyes were still fixed on her. She hadn't been to a taxidermist shop before. But she imagined the stuffed animals there looked something like this. Her fear had ebbed away and given way to something else. Awe. *How on earth is this happening?* she thought.

Then, she had a vision of the mountain range. But this time, her view shifted downwards to the base of the mountain. A solitary figure sat there in the dust. She saw his muscular neck and thick shoulders. The slight perspiration on the back of his sun-browned neck. He exuded an air of calmness, and she drank it in.

Eventually, he looked up, a weathered face wearing black shades. It was as though he saw Rachel and looked right through her at the same time.

As the vision cleared, she watched the panther disintegrate into a cloud of mist before her eyes. She watched the red eyes, sharp teeth, and black paws fade away. Everything was dissolving. In the mist, she saw sparkling shards of light that fell to the floor and fizzled out. It was a dust cloud of tiny fireworks that flashed and died.

Rachel blinked and drew a breath.

She was left staring at nothing. Before her was an empty stairwell.

Rachel curled up into a ball at the foot of the locked basement door. She continued to stare at the flight of stairs, expecting her adversary to reappear. But deep down, she knew someone, somewhere, was watching over her.

12345

IT WAS APPROACHING DAWN. Rachel had not slept at all. She was still curled into a ball at the foot of the basement stairs. She hugged her cardigan around her. The stench of the big cat lingered in her nostrils.

She shivered once and then slowly climbed the stairs. It was a long walk back to the ward on the second floor.

As she ascended, it was as though she was climbing out of a strange dream. Had she been sleepwalking? Had that been a dream? She had once heard about visions. These are where people see things beyond what's in front of them. They see the spiritual world as well. Did that mean she had seen a vision? The only problem was that the reality of the panther chase remained with her.

She wandered back slowly to the second floor. Her legs were heavy. She stumbled along the long corridor that led up to her bed. As she walked, she saw the broken bottles and small pools of medicine. Then she saw the smashed jug of water she had thrown at the panther. This was no vision; it was all real.

The staff were still absent.

Back in the ward, she saw more broken glass on the floor. This was from the broken window that had shattered when the panther jumped into the room.

A large red brick was in the debris. She carefully stepped through the glass and extracted it from the mess. Turning it over in her right hand, she saw some markings on the underside.

The markings showed a tiny imprint of a hand with the little finger missing and some writing. Rachel recoiled. Beneath the hand, she read the words, "Now I've got your attention. Do as I say, or you lose another finger. Await your orders. Don't tell a soul."

Rachel stared at the brick.

It crumbled to dust as she held it. The dust trickled through her fingers and onto the floor. Rachel looked at the red dust on her fingers. She stared wild-eyed at the girls in their beds. She could not believe the girls were still asleep. What was more, where were all the hospital staff? Should she try and wake these people up?

Unable to come to any decisions and feeling exhausted, Rachel climbed back into her bed and waited. She pulled her blanket up to her nose.

Fresh air blew through the broken window.

THE NURSE WOKE her up at eight o'clock for breakfast.

"How on earth did you sleep through that?" she asked

Rachel. "What?" Rachel asked, rubbing her eyes. She saw the broken window. The hospital cleaning staff had cleared up the glass. A dread came over her.

"I don't know why they want to pick on us," the nurse continued.

"Who?" asked Rachel.

"The yobs. Those Zodiacs, you know, the gang that smashed the window. And they left broken glass down the hall. It's a shame, that's what it is: a shame."

"How do you know it was Zodiacs?" asked Rachel.

"Well, it's obvious, isn't it? I don't know. I start my shift at six, and everyone's dozing. Where the security guards were is anyone's guess: probably dozing as well. What do we pay them for? Honestly."

"Did anyone see a big black cat?" Rachel asked her.

"In the hospital?" The nurse gave a half laugh. "No, no cats in here. It would have to be a pretty big one if you ask me. No, I reckon this was done by a gang of lads. Right, my dear, try and eat up your breakfast. You need your strength."

⁓ 12345 ⁓

THE DOCTORS WERE satisfied that Rachel was well enough to be discharged. She was to be treated as an outpatient and come back in a week. She was, of course, welcome to come back at any time or chat with her family doctor. Rachel kept quiet throughout this process, not mentioning the words 'panther' or 'cat' again.

Rachel was happy to leave the hospital, particularly in light of last night's activities. But being sixteen, she had to be discharged to someone, and this caused her a problem. She had no desire to be discharged to her father. Besides, he was probably in the local police station, sitting in a cell.

So, she made up a story about him being her only family and that he couldn't come and pick her up because he was unwell, which was loosely the case. She added that she lived nearby, which was also true, and was happy to walk home.

Fortunately, the junior member of staff who was discharging her seemed convinced by the story and failed to read the notes properly. It also looked like she had a dozen more important things she needed to do, anyway. Rachel didn't volunteer any additional information, either about the social services visit, her father being in a police cell, or anything else, for that matter. She just smiled innocently.

So, Rachel managed to slip through the net and talk and smile her way to freedom.

She didn't want to go back home just yet. It was too weird. What about the incident with her dad? She didn't know if he was still in custody or not. If he was sitting at home, she didn't want to see him.

So, she turned up at Lara's house that Sunday afternoon.

Lara's house was in utter turmoil. There were empty boxes everywhere and flat-packed boxes along the walls, ready to make up. She also saw piles of belongings everywhere she looked.

As soon as Lara opened the front door, Rachel saw things in the hall of this house, which was usually so pristine. Her mum, Cecilia Summer, could be considered house-proud, and this had always been a running joke between the girls. If you moved a sofa, you had to move it back, so the feet were in their indentations on the carpet. If you left the glasses the right way up and not upside down in the cupboard, then you got a stern lecture from Mrs Summer. It was hilarious.

Shortly after some explanation, Rachel was sitting in Lara's bedroom. Lara's mother and father were having a blazing row downstairs. They were arguing about Rachel. The girls heard snatches of the exchange through the floorboards.

"I don't care! She's not staying with us," shrieked Cecilia, who was immaculately made up despite being knee-deep in packing boxes.

"I hear what you're saying, but after all she's been through, I just think…" placated her dad.

"I really don't care right now. We've got a thousand things to do before we catch that plane… can't just take in any…" intoned Lara's mum theatrically.

"Why is this all coming out now? I mean, Lara and Rachel have been friends for…"

"Listen, Gary, I don't care…It's me who'll have to…"

"It will be all right, darling," he soothed.

LARA RAISED her eyebrows and mouthed the word "sorry" to Rachel.

She walked over to the stereo and put on a CD. The music made everything okay again. The two friends sat down on Lara's beanbags. Here was Rachel, with her huge brown eyes and wavy brown hair dyed blue at the tips. There was Lara, who was pale and slim with shoulder-length black hair. They were two friends on two beanbags, together again, with rock music playing in the background. Rachel started to relax. It seemed like a long time since she had experienced anything that resembled normality.

"So, what did happen to your hand, Racoon?" asked Lara. "I told you, Lemur."

"Err, I don't think you did," blurted Lara.

Rachel was Racoon, and Lara was Lemur. Those were their special names for each other. The names seemed to change every few years, depending on what amused them at the time. But Racoon and Lemur were the flavour of the month and had been for some time. Rachel had no idea how it would work when Lara was living in California.

Rachel shrugged. There was so much she wasn't telling her best friend. She sensed that Lara knew this. They had been friends for years and shared almost every thought and every observation. Lara's house had been her place of refuge. It was a place to run to when things got too bad with her dad. But things were changing now, and it was as though Rachel just couldn't stop them from changing. Things were out of her control.

Instead, she said, "Lara, I think I may be losing it."

"I could have told you that. I mean, you were such a wet weekend at the pub on Friday."

"Lara!"

"It's true," snapped Lara.

Rachel looked around the room that had been a haven for her over the years. "This is my room, too," she thought. There were so many shared memories. In the corner, on a pile of clothes, was Lara's matching oversized tee shirt. In a box full of accessories, she saw the photo booth picture of them both. The collection of Sylvanian Families creatures they had both contributed to was sitting by the wall. There were so many memories crammed into one bedroom. It almost made Rachel cry.

"No, I mean, really losing it. Like, totally seeing things and everything," said Rachel.

"What sorts of things?"

"A black panther. Like, in the hospital. No joke. It chased me down the hall and into the basement."

"Sure you weren't dreaming? Did they give you anything for the pain? My dad says they gave him morphine once for his kidney stones, and it made him imagine some, like, really strange things." Lara rolled her eyes to illustrate the point.

Rachel paused and reflected on this.

"I mean, you've been through a lot. What with your dad," Lara went on.

"And my best friend leaving me," whined Rachel, rather more quickly than she'd meant to.

"So, a panther," acknowledged Lara.

"I can still smell it. I can see his teeth. It was so real."

"Like I said, you've been through a lot. I've always meant to ask you, Racoon. Your dad, he can be quite a nutter, right?"

"No, Lara. The answer's no," snapped Rachel.

"But it makes sense – he's drinking, he has a knife. He leaves it outside our house?"

"No, Lara. I'm sure it wasn't like that," insisted Rachel.

"But we've both seen him angry before. He's out of control. He's thrown me out of your house loads of times. And you've always defended him, but can you really tell me honestly that he has never hit you?"

Rachel stared her friend in the face. "My dad has never hit me," she said coldly. "That's why I've never told you; because it has never happened."

She slumped back in her beanbag.

"And I do not believe he cut off my finger," she added. But this was mainly for her own benefit.

Lara got up and moved away, suddenly busying herself with some packing.

☙ 12345 ❧

BY THE EVENING, Rachel had showered, carefully protecting her left hand. It had been a difficult manoeuvre because she wasn't really able to use it for washing. She was now wearing Lara's oversized tee shirt and borrowed a skirt. They always borrowed each other's clothes, so this was nothing new.

Lara came into the bathroom and popped herself onto a wicker clothes basket. She swung her legs.

"Hi, Racoon," she said breezily. "Hi, Lemur."

"Okay, so your dad isn't as bad as I think he is. So, how did you, like, lose the finger?" she asked.

Rachel was brushing her hair in front of the mirror. "I really don't know, Lemur," she said.

Rachel was thinking about the disintegrating brick with the four- fingered hand on it and the message from hell. Or was that all part of her hallucination? What about the man in the mountains? Those mountains were so familiar to her. Where were they? Who on earth was he? Why was he so calm when everything she knew was falling apart?

"I really don't know," she repeated.

IN A SHORT WHILE, it was dinnertime. Apparently, Lara's mum had left the house. She had gone to a friend's. Rachel knew it was because of her, but she really wasn't bothered.

So, Lara's dad, Gary, was in charge. The girls met him at the foot of the stairs. Gary Summer was a tall man with a kind face and greying hair. There was something of the professor about him. In fact, he was a very senior telecoms engineer. He did something like make phone lines work better by using some technology or other. Frankly, it was beyond Rachel, but it sounded pretty neat.

"Hi, girls," he smiled. "I've made pizza and crisps, and there are drinks on the table," sang Gary. "And we've got Ben & Jerry's for dessert. Phish Food, of course."

"Thanks, Dad. I like it when you do the dinner. It's always so much, like, healthier than Mum's," joked Lara.

Her dad smiled sweetly. "You can go through if you want. Just mind my books there. Joel's in there already," he said.

"Oh, and Joel's friend Lake is round for dinner, too. Rachel, you know Lake, don't you?" enquired Gary.

"Yeah," grinned Rachel. "We've met a few times." She turned to Lara, who was giggling.

CHAPTER 6

Daniel Harcourt returned from his business trip. He had been to Mumbai, India. He felt jet-lagged, and the plane journey had been particularly long and tiring. He had flown business class, with its comfortable seats and attentive stewardesses. But despite this, travelling always made him tired.

He placed his suitcase outside the front door, let his shoulders slump, and fished for his keys in his leather rucksack. The gargoyle doorknocker stared at him.

His wife was at work. His children were at school.

Daniel was a very skilful senior software architect with a large multinational computer company. He had set up some intricate and successful computer systems for a number of high-paying clients: banks, big pharma, questionable governments.

Home at last, Daniel pushed open the door. He breathed in the familiar smell of his house: freshly cut flowers.

His last trip had kept him away from home for a fortnight. He knew these trips were getting too long now. He barely saw his family when he was working in England, his own country. But when he was away, he saw more of his team than he did his wife. It was a high price to pay for this lifestyle. But then, this lifestyle demanded a high price.

He had chosen this path, no one else.

❧ 12345 ❧

Daniel washed his face in his bedroom sink. He was standing in a large red and golden room. There was a view of a massive garden with a long drive leading up to a pair of wrought-iron gates. He liked the gates because they kept the world out. They also kept his world in.

His suitcase was open on the king-size bed behind him.

"You're looking old," Daniel thought to himself. His face was lined and weathered. His eyes were red and sunken. His thinning hair was shabby and needed a cut.

As he looked at his red eyes, a familiar voice rang out in his head. It was a voice from the past and one which he hadn't heard for a long time.

"Daniel William Harcourt," it moaned slowly. The voice had a metallic ring, like the chiming of a distant church bell.

Daniel froze and stared into the mirror. "Daniel William Harcourt," it rang out again.

"No. It can't be," uttered Daniel. He saw his red eyes widen in the mirror.

In seconds, he tumbled back into a long-forgotten past. It was a past of fear and paranoia.

❧ 12345 ❧

Once upon a time, Daniel had wanted to know what was on the other side. Some people would say he was obsessed. It was partly the darkness he was drawn to. But even more attractive was the idea of having power over other people.

He craved having power over those who pushed him around. He wanted revenge on those who were cruel to him, merciless in fact. He wanted to beat the bullies in his life, his schoolmasters, and his classmates. He also wanted revenge on his domineering parents, particularly his father.

His father ruled with a rod of steel, and Daniel wanted him to pay for his years of cruelty. As a bonus, he wanted to get a particular girl to fall in love with him. She ignored him and treated him like a nonentity, but it made him love her all the more.

Becoming an initiate into the occult, the dark arts, seemed the only solution. He learned that if you found out how to harness the power of the dark angels, they would do your bidding. There was so much to learn, and he had the brains to learn it. He embarked upon the path to 'the higher knowledge' with relish.

That was how he met his friend Samyaza.

Samyaza was an ancient one, one of the Grigori, or 'Watchers.' Samyaza came as a friendly spirit guide to Daniel, appearing as a beautiful young girl with long flowing hair and full red lips. He was instantly smitten. He enjoyed her company when she was with him, inhabiting his spirit. He thought about her when she was away.

The first year was thrilling as Samyaza showed Daniel a world beyond his imaginings. It was full of power, adventure, and hidden knowledge. He learned about incantations and spell casting, shape-shifting, and sorcery. These were beautiful things that other people were just too dull to grasp, so he thought.

He saw his world fall to its knees before him. It was then that he won and courted Arabella Samantha, the beautiful girl who was the object of his affection.

Her name was a soothing balm to his mind. Attracting her to him was the result of long hours of occult studying and spell casting. She was dating someone else, so he worked hard in the spiritual realms to rid her of the other suitor. His young rival soon experienced ill health and fell by the wayside. Arabella lost interest and gravitated towards Daniel. It was all worth it.

His life changed when he gained the love of Arabella. He decided to walk away from the dark arts.

But Samyaza was a jealous mistress and soon showed her true colours – or his true colours, as it turned out. Daniel learned that everything has a cost. Samyaza was, in reality, a disfigured old demon, cantankerous and curmudgeonly at best. He appeared in Daniel's spirit at the drop of a hat and frequently outstayed his welcome. There was no escaping Samyaza or his demands.

The subsequent years were shrouded in great darkness for Daniel as Samyaza exacted a higher and higher price from him. Rather than harnessing the power of a dark angel, Daniel had been ensnared himself.

By day, he lived an apparently normal life with his true love, Arabella Samantha. He made her Mrs Daniel William Harcourt, and they had children: two boys. But in secret, he served Samyaza and did his bidding. In public, he was a devoted father and husband. By night, he was a monster: manipulated, used, and in chains.

His master's bidding varied from casting spells to carrying out theft and actual physical harm. This continued for several years. At that time, the children, Cameron and little Rory were just babies.

⚜ *1*2345 ⚜

ONE DAY, he went to a remote place and screamed at his master until he was hoarse. He poured out his fury and his hate.

When he returned to the house, things had changed. In both his head and his polluted spirit, things seemed lighter. How he had shaken free of Samyaza was a mystery to him.

He carried on with his life, and it was wonderful. He left the spell-casting and wizardry behind him and walked away. His career soared, even without the occult practices. He got the house, the cars, the foreign travel, and private schooling for the children, all without wielding the dark arts. His wife wore only the best. He enjoyed privately catered dinner parties with influential friends. The best part was that it was he who had achieved it – Daniel William Harcourt.

He'd achieved it all on his own.

❧ 12345 ❧

"DANIEL WILLIAM HARCOURT," the voice was saying for a third time. "I'm here, Samyaza," said Daniel resignedly. "Why are you back?"

"Oh, Daniel. I never left," professed Samyaza, his decrepit form appearing in Daniel's spirit. The fallen angel smiled a horrible smile.

"Now I've got your attention, await your orders. There's a good chap," warned Samyaza. He grinned and showed his blackened teeth.

Daniel watched as the Watcher made himself invisible again.

❧ 12345 ❧

THE POLICE HAD RELEASED Rachel's father without charge. He had been held and questioned for a number of hours. Most of the hours were dedicated to making him stew and sobering him up. It was a common police tactic. But in the end, the police could find no link between the kitchen knife and Rachel's blood. They also found no motive for such an attack on her person. They found no evidence of an attack by the father on the daughter. So, they were forced to accept his story and see him as a man who was anxious for the safety of his child.

So, the police had the complete story, as told by Edward Race. Mr Race insisted he had passed out on his floor on the far side of the bed. He had been drinking all evening: whiskey and lots of it. He had heard his daughter Rachel's screams but had found it difficult to rouse himself. When he finally managed to do this, he went into her room and switched on the light. She was gone. He saw the blood and panicked.

Then he went down to the kitchen to grab a weapon. He found the kitchen knife and ran outside, thinking he heard Rachel's attacker fleeing. He had drunk a lot of alcohol, and this had clouded his decision-making.

Outside, it was dark. He made a circuit of the house and then saw his daughter walking away from the house and down the street. He called out to her because he feared she was hurt.

When she carried on walking, he believed she was scared and wanted to reassure her. He ran after her to check she was all right. But when he got to the park, he was unable to explain himself because he was so out of breath he found it hard to speak. She ran on.

At Rachel's friends' house, where the Summer family lived, Edward Race finally caught up with his daughter. This is the point when he dropped the knife and caught his daughter. Then he called the emergency services.

The Griffton police decided not to pursue the matter but had a stern word with Mr Race about his drinking and responsibilities as a parent. They were keen to involve social services in his family life. But they would relent if he pledged to become a better father.

Chastened, he returned home.

That was yesterday. Rachel got a brief synopsis of her dad's story from the police, who had gotten her mobile number from her father.

She texted her dad and said: "Coming home."

HER FATHER WAS WAITING in the doorway as she approached the house. Without a word, she walked past him, avoiding his eyes. She sat down on the sofa and folded her arms.

"Let's see your finger then," demanded Eddie. Reluctantly, she held out her bandaged hand. "Hmm," said her father.

After a long pause, Rachel spat out, "You didn't call me? Not even to see how I was?"

Her father stood stony-faced. He wasn't in the habit of showing his emotions except when he was drinking. The only emotion he trusted himself to show was anger.

"Not even a text?" she asked.

"Look, love," he implored. "I was in the nick, wasn't I?"

"And afterwards?" she asked.

He turned away. Instead, he said, "So what happened? To your finger, I mean."

"Well, if it wasn't you, then I don't know who…"

"Me? You really thought it was me who did that? Look at me, Rachel. Do you really think I'm capable of that? Me?"

She stared at the carpet. He had cleared away the bottles and papers that had lain across the floor of the front room.

The curtains were half drawn.

"I mean, I know we've had our moments, but… Look at me, Rachel."

Slowly, she lifted her eyes. In front of her was a big man, a strong man. Her father, whom she often feared and rarely understood.

He had tears in his eyes.

As their eyes locked, he crumpled before her and put his big arms around her.

"Whoever's done this to my baby will pay," he promised.

"Don't, Dad," begged Rachel.

In his throat, she heard the beginnings of a sob.

Rachel put her hands on her father's shoulders. She fought back her own tears. "I'm staying at Lara's for a few days," she whispered.

"But…"

"She's leaving for America soon," she added. "I want to spend time with her. I came back to get some stuff."

The doorbell rang.

Slowly, Rachel's father rose up to his full height and opened the door. He was expecting the police, social services, or the press.

He wasn't expecting the six eyes that stared back at him.

Lara, Lara's brother Joel, and his friend Lake stood together and peered at him as though he were an animal at the zoo.

"Yes?" he growled.

"We're here to see Rachel," chimed Lara.

"Right. You two stay out there. You can come in," he ordered Lara, taking control.

As Lara slid into the room, he closed the front door on the boys.

THEY WERE UP in Rachel's bedroom.

Her dad had stripped the bed and changed the sheets. He had cleaned up as best he could. It was still her room, with her possessions and unique design style. She was familiar with every poster and book, item of clothing, and pretty ornament. But looking around the room, Rachel knew that everything had changed.

There were no clues at all to suggest who or what had taken her finger. The mystery of it had settled into her bones and was now a deeply rooted part of her.

Lara was clearly spooked, but helped her grab her essentials and pack them into a small pink rucksack.

Wide-eyed, Lara asked, "So this is where it happened?" Rachel grunted.

"Racoon, right here? You were lying right here, and then, what? You woke up, and your finger was gone?"

"That's right, Lemur."

"You didn't see anyone? No one?"

Rachel took a handful of bracelets and neck chains and the book she was reading.

She glanced at her friend. "No one," she insisted.

Lara stared one more time at the bed, the floor, the window, and the bed again. Then they nodded to each other and headed out.

On the way out of the house, Rachel passed her father, who was sitting on the sofa, trying to appear nonchalant.

"I want you to do something for me, Dad," she implored with her new boldness. It was the boldness of someone who had got right to the edge and survived.

"I want you to see someone about the booze. Properly this time," she demanded.

"Okay," he murmured quietly.

She opened the door and smiled at Lake Emerson, who was standing behind Joel.

CHAPTER 7

Nepal. The Himalayan Mountains.

The Himalayan Mountain range stretches across five nations, sprinkling a hundred mountain peaks over China, India, Nepal, Pakistan, and Bhutan.

Caleb emerged from his tent early in the morning. It was a cool day in the mountains. He breathed in a lungful of air and then another and stretched up to the sky.

Lifting his eyes to the mountain slopes, Caleb Noble saw the ridges of snow he had left behind a few days earlier.

"The abode of snow," he stated. Himalaya is a Sanskrit name that means 'the abode of snow,' and he liked the idea that there was a place where snow lived.

Down in the foothills where he stood, it was drier. He still saw a flurry of snow every so often, but not the blizzards he had been greeted with on the higher slopes.

It was a beautiful new day. A cool breeze blew.

Caleb's muscular arms rippled as his forearms, biceps, triceps, and deltoids elongated beneath a white tee-shirt. His tent was a rugged brown and orange affair, weathered and strong, like himself.

He had come to the mountains to hear them moan and

boom. It was phenomenal, unlike anything he had met until now.

Caleb knew what was ahead and wanted to witness the beginning. *This moment is unique,* thought Caleb. *Actually, every moment is unique. But this moment is also profound. In time, it might be too difficult to return here,* he thought.

The Initiation had occurred. Everything had changed.

He ran a large hand through his short-cropped grey hair and smiled up a 'good morning' to the heavens. He was confident things would be all right in the end. He was as confident of this as he was on the ground he walked on or in the sun that rose in the sky. He was also confident things would get far worse before they got better.

It was time to move on after one final coffee.

He stood at the base of Makalu, the fifth-highest mountain in the world. He was just twenty-two kilometres east of Mount Everest. That was where the sun was rising to preside over a cold white sky. It shone over the head of Everest and its siblings, sending a yellow glow across their broad, snowy planes.

Makalu stood on its own: a perfect four-sided pyramid. Massive, immovable, and majestic was Makalu striding Nepal and Tibet. Rising just north of the higher summit, separated by a narrow saddle, was Chomo Lonzo, a subsidiary peak of Makalu.

The mountain had proved through history to be a challenging climb. Only five of its first sixteen attempts were successful. It sat in the Khumbu region among many other giants, unassailable until 1955.

For climbers, Makalu is viewed as one of the most difficult mountains in the world to ascend. It is known for its steep cliff faces and knife-edged ridges that are completely open to the elements.

Caleb had made the climb through sheer perseverance and the grace of God.

He was now some distance from the mountains because the

approach was so long. But from his vantage point, he could hear the mountain moan.

He lit his stove.

Soon, he had a good, strong cup of black coffee. He drank it down to the grounds and ate a hunk of dry bread, sitting cross-legged on the ground.

"This is good," he rejoiced.

Nearby was a bowl of *daal bhaat*, the remains of creamy daal and rice from the day before, covered in a layer of ice.

12345

CALEB HAD PACKED up his tent and stood ankle-deep in fresh snow a little further up the path. He had to go up before he could go down, and this meant more snow. He strapped his rucksack onto his back and shivered.

He noticed that the Sherpas had made themselves scarce. Their tents were gone, and they were nowhere to be seen. His Sherpa companions had been good company, and he had enjoyed the cook's culinary skills. Caleb squinted and scanned the white horizon, seeing nothing of note.

Tumlingtar would be at least a week away. It was a long hike out of the belly of the wild mountains and the ice, but that was Caleb's next destination. He centred his pack and walked purposefully on.

12345

ON SEVERAL OCCASIONS, while trekking through the arid and barren Himalayan valleys, Caleb had spotted a solitary watchman. It was always the same. It would be a small man dressed in white, standing and staring until Caleb physically turned his head to acknowledge him. Then he would run like the wind, head down, away into the distance. Caleb observed him racing west across the empty landscape until the watchman became a dot. This happened every few days.

The path became greener as he descended further into the valleys. On the way to Tumlingtar, Caleb spotted a couple of medieval Hindu temples. They were either wide and long or tall and layered, with spiky peaks. They tended to be abandoned, although there were signs that several of them were supplied with fresh flowers and generally cared for. Around them were huge forests of rhododendrons, Nepal's national flower. Their dazzling beauty exploded onto the scene.

Amidst the forest of flowers, Caleb spied a watchman.

CALEB CROSSED over the Arun River and hiked the trail from Num to Khandbari. He faced a descent from the mountains, which was very steep at times. It took him several thousand feet down into the lower hills.

It was hot all year round in the lower hills, where most of the villagers lived. Caleb soon felt warm from his exertion. He paused several times to watch Everest receding to the west. He pictured Tibet moving ever further from him as he ventured south.

From Khandbari, he crossed over to Chainpur, a bright and gleaming village with clean streets and smart little lodges. Chainpur is famous for its brass, and brass was everywhere. Children ate farm-fresh oranges and chattered with each other noisily. A hill led down to Tumlingtar, the region's only airport. Caleb rested by a wall and took in his surroundings. He gazed at a small elementary school and the large grassy compound outside it.

Soon, he was eating cooked rice and Tarkari – a selection of vegetable curries – and sipping tea in one of the few cafés. Young men and women stared through the glassless window at the tall Westerner and giggled amongst themselves.

Caleb smiled and took in their friendly and open faces. They were beautiful people, beautifully designed, with black hair, smooth faces, and shiny dark eyes. Then he spotted a face in the crowd which bore marks of malice.

The watchman noted him and ducked away, slipping away around the corner.

Caleb knew it was time to move on.

He paid the café owner and left the café with his rucksack and pack balanced across his shoulders. Walking past the brass-clad buildings, he scanned to the left and the right, looking for anything unusual. The young people had grown bored with him and had wandered off, and the weather outside was warm and pleasant. He decided to go for a stroll in the general direction of the hill that led down to Tumlingtar. Something told him this would not be a straightforward venture.

Walking between two buildings, he found himself in a court-yard in the middle of a group of dwellings. On the far side, between the two buildings opposite, he was faced with one of his adversaries.

This was not a watchman dressed in white, with a sly face and swift foot. No, this was a tall and robust Sapana, or 'Dream Fighter,' who carried a long cane and a scowl.

Caleb froze.

The Dream Fighter's eyes glowed red, and he immediately began to advance on Caleb. Although Caleb was muscular, his adversary had the advantages of height as well as brawn. Plus, he did not have the hindrance of a pack on his back. Caleb quickly calculated his options.

Calmly, he walked back out between the two buildings the way he had come and into the village streets. Then he walked round a corner and re-entered the courtyard, but this time from another angle. He passed through where the Dream Fighter had first stood and walked on, finding the long way around to the hill down to Tumlingtar. His unusual manoeuvre had confused the Dream Fighter, who was presumably trying to find him in the main body of the village.

Caleb didn't look back.

On the side of the road was a scattering of dark brown trees with thick trunks. He felt it was time to leave the main road and enter the covering of the trees. It was also cooler here. He walked on down the hill.

Eventually, with Tumlingtar in sight, Caleb came face to face with another Sapana Dream Fighter. This one wore a red and black sash, and his expression was like the rumbling of thunder. He stood in the middle of the path ahead with his arms folded and a tree on either side. His feet were planted firmly into the fallen leaves. He also held a sharp staff diagonally across his body, under his thick arms.

Caleb paused.

Suddenly, another two Dream Fighters appeared to his right and left. One was in black, with a large red mark on his head, and the other in red and brown leather. They walked forward, palms open, aiming to pin Caleb between them. He glanced behind him and saw another one in the distance, but approaching fast. It was the Dream Fighter from the village who had stood before him in the courtyard.

Caleb raised his eyes to the treetops and then sat down on the ground. As he sat, his pack rested on the ground, level with the bottom of his back. The men prepared to converge on Caleb, with the Dream Fighter in front unfolding his arms and readying his cane.

Then Caleb closed his eyes.

CHAPTER 8

Sitting in the middle of the woods on the hill to Tumlingtar, Caleb spoke to his master, the creator of the heavens and the earth. He felt the presence of the Dunamis, and an answer formed inside him. It spoke just one phrase, but Caleb heard two things, as was often the case. "Do not be anxious about anything" was the first, and "I have already overcome the world" was the second.

The Dunamis was the source of power the creator had left to equip those who had pledged their allegiance to him. Caleb made it a point to walk in step with the Dunamis, and the Dunamis led and protected him. It was a beautiful relationship and one full of adventure.

Perfectly calm, he opened his eyes to see the four Sapana Dream Fighters lying on their backs before him.

He breathed in the fragrant scent of the forest.

The large, muscular men lay rigid, staring at the high branches with patches of blue sky peeping through.

Caleb raised his eyes to the treetops again. "Thank you, Dunamis, my friend," he said.

He then looked long and hard at the men around him, who

were unable to move. He knew they only lived because the creator had decided to sustain them with his breath.

If he decided not to sustain the world one day, it would blink out of existence. It was as simple as that.

"Who is your master?" he called out.

"Our master is Samyaza," chanted the Dream Fighters. Caleb pondered this for a long time.

"Your master is Samyaza, the father of the Nephilim?"

"The same," they affirmed. Caleb was speaking in English while the men spoke in their native tongue. The Dunamis was translating for them.

"Thank you for your cooperation. In return, I am going to give you a taste of freedom if you want it," informed Caleb. "What you do then is up to you," he added.

He rose to his feet, slipping off his pack. It fell to the ground off his broad shoulders. Then he lunged slowly towards the Dream Fighter in front of him and extracted the man's staff. It was a fine piece of wood, crafted into a beautiful weapon, steely and strong with an ornate spine. Shapes and runes were etched into the cane and were stained a darker brown.

Caleb raised the cane. He whipped it through the air before bringing it down hard towards the heart of the supine warrior. He stopped short of the man's body. Then he tapped it lightly on the man's red and black sash at the last minute.

"Do you want this taste of freedom?" he asked the man. The man stared at him and then nodded.

Caleb roared, "By the power of the Dunamis, be freed. Any hold over you by Samyaza and his cohorts is broken. If you choose to go back to him, then that's your choice, and you must take the consequences."

The large Dream Fighter, dressed in black, groaned. He let his head fall back into a pile of leaves. He closed his eyes and grinned, tasting freedom from Samyaza for the very first time. Then his body went limp as though he had slipped into a nice warm bath.

Caleb asked his question to each of them, all of whom seemed to be eager for the 'gift' that was on offer.

He turned to his right, tapping the next man with the cane. This one was dressed in red and brown leather, with a thick leather area at the front.

"You are free. Samyaza and his gang have no power over you," he claimed with authority.

Then he smiled. "My friends, this is a clean slate, but be warned, Samyaza will return to you soon and demand to know your loyalty. What you do, what you tell him, is your choice."

The fighter on the right exhaled. He brought his hands to his chest as though he had been struck in the heart. Caleb turned to the other side and carried out a similar operation. Then he wheeled around and brought the cane down on the fighter behind him.

"You, my friend from the village," whispered Caleb, "Samyaza has no hold, no power over you, and in the name of the Dunamis, be freed." The Dream Fighter from Chainpur coughed loudly and bounced a foot off the ground. Then he lay still, twitching and smiling. Caleb raised his eyebrows.

By this time, the man in front was sitting up and scratching his head. The others were also returning to themselves.

"Listen carefully to me," Caleb called out. He picked up his pack and began to fix it back on, one arm at a time. "Today, a power greater than Samyaza has come to you. Samyaza will return to you and try to bind you up again. I urge you to resist him. Call on the power of the Dunamis, and he will protect you. Now, you have tasted true freedom. That fiend no longer owns you. Remember my words. They will be life to you."

Caleb picked a path to the right of the big man in front of him. As he passed, he handed him his ornate staff.

Nothing hindered his journey between the trees now. He was free to travel down the hill to Tumlingtar. Soon, he would be back at the airport, where he would trade his climbing gear for more comfortable clothes and provisions.

Then, he would meet the prophetess at the appointed time and place.

He never doubted he would.

CALEB ARRIVED AT BALI AIRPORT. His flight from Jakarta was pleasant and interesting. He had eaten a hot vegetable curry and rice that could rival any restaurant. Caleb travelled in a small tubular plane with a large number of Indonesian business travellers and a handful of American tourists. It appeared he was the only European.

He had been enjoying the sounds of the conversations around him and digging into his curry. But then, halfway through the meal, the Dunamis had given him some words to share with the passenger beside him. The passenger was a small black-haired man in a light grey suit.

This time, Caleb spoke in fluent Indonesian to the man. He had no idea what he was saying, not being a native speaker himself. It was, as ever, a mind-boggling experience for Caleb. But it was not the first time he had spoken in a language that was not his own. Caleb looked directly into the man's eyes and delivered the message, slightly surprised at the sounds that came out of his mouth. It was a beautifully expressive language.

As he spoke, Caleb's face began to glow with the power of the Dunamis.

The man listened, his eyes widening by the second. Then, just when Caleb thought his eyes couldn't open any wider, the man began to cry.

"Thank you, thank you," he muttered repeatedly. He wasn't crying tears of pain but of relief.

Caleb smiled and returned to his food, leaving his companion lost in thought. Then Caleb slept.

When they arrived at the airport, they departed from the plane and never saw each other again.

SMALL BOXES the size of a child's hand were strewn across the pavement of the Balinese streets. Inside the boxes were colourful flower sacrifices. The locals were begging their gods for mercy and favour. Some laid their flower sacrifices to beg and others to appease the gods. They were pleading with them to withhold their anger. It was a daily burden for many people.

The heat of this place was intense, and it was a massive contrast to Nepal with its icy mountains. Caleb felt twice as heavy as before. This was even though he had quartered the weight of his pack by selling his climbing gear and tent back in Tumlingtar.

As he wandered along an ocean path, he took in the mass of huge green-leaved vegetation, bright posters, and spiky temples. The blue water shimmered, dazzling in the sunlight.

The sun fired up every colour and made it luminescent.

Past a collection of spiky palms, scratching at the sky, he saw tourist boats drifting out to hidden islands. At the nearby shore, he saw the wide areas where the Balinese harvested seaweed to sell to the Chinese. They raked it out of the sea and spread it out to dry under the intense sunlight: fields of green tentacles that faded to brown.

TRACING THE COAST, high above the sea, Caleb watched the waves and thought about the view of the earth he had seen from the ridges of Makalu. High in the mountains, he had witnessed the curvature of the earth.

THE PROPHETESS WAS a woman in her forties, an American dressed in a summer dress with tiny flowers on it. Her face was lightly sunburned, and her roughly tied hair had been bleached white by the sun.

Her name was Serena.

Caleb had found her in a village and been directed straight to her door by the Dunamis. She lived in a simple stone-walled cottage, which had a wooden boat and a bicycle leaning against it. Her garden was beautifully tended and had a pool of purple and pink flowers at the centre.

"You are Caleb," she stated.

He nodded and started to take his pack off his back.

"Walk with me," she added.

He shrugged the pack back onto his shoulders and smiled. "You've travelled far?"

"Nepal. The mountains," he told her.

"I see." She stared into the distance with her dark brown eyes. It was late afternoon now, though the heat showed little sign of abating.

"There's a little hotel down this way where you can stay. You must be hungry. They have wonderful coconut fish, fresh from the bay. We will talk there."

He nodded. He slipped on his black sunglasses, sensing the conversation had reached its natural end.

After all, he was more than used to dwelling in silence.

"A LITTLE HOTEL?" asked Caleb. The white stone complex was majestic, with its red wooden walkways that soared above broad plants and still water. Paper-doily crocuses and white lilies floated on the surface. On either side of the wooden bridges, feathery leaves fanned out, catching the rays. They were reminiscent of office roller blinds.

"And this will cost me how much?" enquired Caleb. "I know the owner," smiled Serena.

THE FISH WAS DELICIOUS, just as Serena had promised. She talked to her friend while Caleb ate alone. The owner was a small and round man with a large smile and a bald head. His wife and kids all worked with him. He had made Caleb feel very welcome and given him the best room in the house. This was a great blessing, as far as Caleb was concerned. He had been living for far too long in his brown tent. The thought of sleeping in a proper bed was most appealing.

Serena had suggested he stay for a few days to recuperate and make the most of the sun before he moved on. If the time was right to rest for a few days, he would do that. But if it was not, he was content to find another tent to sleep in with nothing but a sleeping bag, a sheet of canvas, and a roll mat between him and the ground.

This was the life he had been called to, after all.

THERE WERE a few guests at the hotel, but they mostly stayed in their groups and drank cocktails by the bar. Caleb grabbed a fruit drink and walked out with the prophetess onto a wooden balcony. They went to a table overlooking the sea. They were talking about names.

"In Bali, you can describe a person in at least six ways, you know," explained Serena.

"Tell me more," said Caleb.

"So, you've got your personal name, which everyone has. Children are the ones most likely to be called by their personal names, which are given to them on their first birthday. Then you've got a name that describes where you are in the family and which number child you are. Another name links you with your family members. This is kind of cool because great-grandparents and great-grandchildren are both called *kumpi* and are considered to be part of the same generation. It's linked to the concept of reincarnation. Then you have a name that tells of your children, so for you, your mother would be 'mother of Caleb.'"

Caleb smiled.

"Then you can have a name for your social caste and a name for your occupation. Six names. Oh, I nearly forgot – you might also have a name for your clan."

"That's a lot of names."

"It sure is. Now, I believe you are looking for a name, right?" asked Serena.

"That's right. One name, and then I sense I am to travel north to find the name," whispered Caleb, half to himself.

Serena looked out across the ocean.

"It's started, hasn't it? The Initiation," said Serena softly. "In the mountains. The Dunamis told me."

Caleb made no response. They sat in silence for a while, watching the same sunset today as had set yesterday and every day that preceded it. Bali was beautiful. Spectacular, in fact. The place seemed ageless, trapped in time, with its colours and smells preserved for eternity.

"Her name," whispered Serena, "is Rachel Race."

CHAPTER 9

It was a week later. Lara was going to be gone in three more. Rachel sighed and thumbed through a stack of CDs, painfully aware of her missing finger as she flipped through the plastic squares. The painkillers they had given her at the hospital seemed to be successful in dulling the sharp pain at the base of her little finger.

She was forever sorting the disks into alphabetical order, but as mindless tasks went, she rather enjoyed it. She got to look at the album art and refresh her mental catalogue. Iona was playing a random selection of boy band tunes from the past decade, and Rachel's mind was drifting pleasantly.

There was always something to do at Rock and Shock, she thought, and Ben was such a great manager. Where else could you work, hang out, listen to music, play about with vinyl records and CDs, see your friends, and talk about nothing?

Rachel had volunteered to help out with the midweek stock take for a couple of days. It took place on Tuesday and Wednesday, but after that, Ben had offered her three days a week. That was until she decided what she was going to do with her life. Rachel was perfectly happy to work with Ben and Iona for the rest of her life. She would be content to play the latest tunes and just exist.

The midweek stock take had been such great fun. They were sitting on the floor. Rachel, Ben, Iona, and Anju, a temp Ben, had got in for the job. Stacks of CDs and records towered around them, and Ben punched numbers into his laptop.

Iona had brought in several bottles of Coke and cider, and Ben had bought loads of snacks, including chocolate chip cookies and crisps. There was more than enough for the four of them. Rachel thought he was a genius, making a stock take into a party. If she ever had a shop, that was exactly what she would do to motivate her staff. Even though they stayed late into the night, they didn't notice the time go by because they were having such great fun.

By the second day, they were done, and so they cranked up the volume on the stereo and finished the cider. It was a classic.

Number one, it was a great party, thought Rachel. Number two, it kept her out of the house. Things weren't so bad with her father at the moment, and they had found some sort of level since the incident. Saying that they tended to avoid each other and do their own thing. Number three, Rachel loved hanging out with Iona, who was four years older and super cool. She didn't even miss spending time with Lara, who was busy with her packing and planning for the move most of the time. Honestly, how much packing does one family have to do?

ON THE FINAL night of the stock take, she had that dream again. It was the one about the mountains.

She was an eagle flying above the mountains and staring into the grey shadows in the folds of the brilliant white slopes. Hard-edged fissures tore vertical stripes down the length of the mountain, and a layer of cloud hung around its middle. She soared above the mountain into the deep blue sky. As she cast her beady eagle eyes about the mountain ridges and saw the curvature of the earth below, she heard the mountain groan. It was a deep-bellied groan, full of pain, anguish, and torment, no longer a moan as before.

Then, the mountain range began to roar.

Rachel extended the tips of her wings as far as they would go. She executed a right-hand turn and wheeled off into the sky.

SHE'D SEEN him around before, hanging around outside the shop.

She thought he might have had an eye for Iona, though he was more likely to be craving company from anyone. But this time, the homeless man had been staring through the window for close to an hour, with eyes that resembled ET the Extra Terrestrial's. His matted beard and long hair needed a thorough cleaning. It also looked like he layered on a new garment whenever he got hold of one rather than letting anything go. Every so often, he gesticulated in the air and jerked his neck. He was holding a never-ending conversation with himself.

By mid-morning, he was in the shop, clattering the CD cases and staring across the shop at Iona and Rachel. As he looked, he shuffled the CDs and put them back in the wrong places. He even dropped a few on the floor.

"That guy's making a complete nuisance of himself," lamented Iona, her eyes wide open. "We really should do something, though I don't really want to go near him myself." Her voice was breathy and light.

"Why don't you go in the back and get Ben?" whispered Rachel. "I'll stay out here and watch that he doesn't grab anything and run."

"What will you do if he does?"

"I don't know."

Iona lingered next to Rachel, undecided about leaving her alone.

Meanwhile, across the shop, the tall vagrant continued to clatter the CD cases and mutter to himself. Rachel and Iona, both standing behind the counter, eyed him for a little while longer.

"Okay, I'm going to get Ben," stated Iona as decisively as she was ever going to. Then, she disappeared through the doorway.

It wasn't a huge shop by any means. It was actually a converted house with an extended front room. The back rooms led through a maze of utility rooms to Ben's office at the back of the building. The bedrooms had become storerooms. Each wall was covered in IKEA shelves, and the kitchen was now another storage area with tea-making facilities.

Ben was planning to extend the shopping area through to the other rooms. But if he did, he would have to face both storage and security issues.

For the time being, the shop was well-designed, and anyone at the counter had a clear view across the shop and out through the windows into the street and the sea beyond.

For Rachel, this meant she could watch today's visitor, protected by half a dozen heavy racks of CDs.

The seconds ticked by with no sign of Iona. Rachel kept her eye on the man whilst glancing down at the phone.

By the time the police came, it could be too late.

The man smelled of alcohol and stale body odour. He was muttering about someone who was out to get him, by the sounds of it. Suddenly, from across the room, he called out, "So what happened to your finger?"

"How do you know about that?" demanded Rachel hoarsely, hearing her words coming out far too loudly. Where was Iona, and why hadn't she found Ben yet?

Then she realised she still wore the packing around the stump of her finger and felt stupid. Anyone could see her hand and make a comment like that. It was obvious.

"If you're not going to buy anything, we'd like you to leave the store," demanded Rachel as forcefully as she could. She decided to say 'we' rather than 'I' so that she didn't make it too personal.

The man stood and stared for a while, with his head to one side. He had long, lank hair, matted and twisted, with long sideburns down his face. She glanced at his dirty fingernails.

"Samyaza's got your finger," whispered the man through his beard. He grinned and put his forefinger to his lips, making a shushing sound.

"What?" entreated Rachel. She gaped like a fish. "Who?"

Just then, the man grabbed a handful of DVDs from a side shelf and turned to go. Ben and Iona came striding out from the back of the shop. They saw him turn and run.

"You okay, Rach?" shouted Ben, as he began to give chase. "I'm fine. I think," she yelped.

As he fled, the man dropped the DVDs across the floor, leaving a trail from the shelf to the doorway.

Ben rushed out of his shop, looking down the road to the right, where the man had gone. But it was too late. He had disappeared into Griffton's maze of streets.

⌒12345⌒

LAKE EMERSON WAS DOING a Saturday shift at the Griffton News. It wasn't a bad job at all. He'd left school after the sixth form, but unfortunately, his A-level grades weren't fantastic because he had messed about a bit too much.

That meant he didn't have any further qualifications. He had ideally needed a journalism diploma from somewhere. But he knew this probably wasn't going to happen, at least not unless he retook his A levels, and he wasn't prepared to do that.

His dream job was to be a news reporter. His mum said that one way into the business was to offer his services as a junior research assistant at the Griffton News, assisting the other writers and editors. That way, he could learn the ropes, make some contacts, and get the chance to write a news story one day. He'd live at home, and his parents would help him out for money until he got onto his own two feet, of course.

So here he was, working in the offices of the busiest paper for miles around. It was the main read for the families and businesses of this coastal city, with a circulation of around a hundred thousand.

He was working on a story about a local shipping company that was treating their staff badly, according to a whistleblower who worked there. Lake knew they had to go carefully for several reasons. Reason one was the shipping company was an advertiser. Reason two was that the whistleblower had a young family to think of. Reason three was the shipping company was likely to pursue legal action if the story didn't stick to the facts.

It was giving Lake a headache, but he had managed to find some great contacts in the industry and also a goldmine of financial irregularities, which cast the brothers who owned the business in a very poor light.

As he wandered over to the photocopier with a handful of papers, he passed the desk of Tracy, a blonde-haired girl in the art and production department who was a couple of years older than him. He tried not to notice her unbuttoning the top of her white blouse as he passed her. But she caught his eye.

Lake felt flustered but continued to walk towards the photocopier. He was looking forward to his lunch break. He had planned to pass by Rock and Shock, check the latest drum and bass releases, and see if Rachel Race was in.

Now this.

Tracy opened a conversation. "So, you like to skate, don't you?"

"Yeah, I skate," mumbled Lake, avoiding her eyes. Tracy was beautiful, and he could easily get ensnared by her, but he also had Rachel on his mind.

There was something about Rachel. She was an enigma: so

complicated and interesting. So troubled. They had got together a couple of times the past couple of weeks, along with Lara and Joel, and he had found himself drawn to her. Beyond that cute face and big brown eyes, and the wavy brown and blue hair was someone he really wanted to spend time researching.

Tracy looked back at her screen, and Lake managed to glance at his watch. Ten minutes to lunchtime.

"So, what are you doing later on?" whispered Tracy. She licked her lips and waited for Lake to take the bait.

"I've got plans," he muttered.

RACHEL TOOK her lunch break on time, wandered out of the shop, and headed along the seafront. Iona had to do some grocery shopping, so Rachel was on her own for an hour or so.

It was a mild summer's day, with the really hot weather due to arrive in a few weeks. Lara would miss the heat, but then again, she would be in California, where it was hot all the time.

The beach was full of tourists hanging out and locals taking a break from work. Children played with buckets and spades, and flecks of colour filled the horizon as bathers plunged into the sea. High above, seagulls whirled and swirled, alighting on discarded scraps of food from time to time and emitting that piercing screech.

Rachel put her hands in the pockets of her jeans and set off towards town. Twenty minutes of walking would get her there, near the offices of the Griffton News.

Maybe it was a little bit crazy, but last Wednesday, during her lunch break, she hiked up to the centre of town just to stand outside the tower where Lake worked. She'd grabbed a sandwich and sat on a park bench, watching the newspaper tower, and then walked back down to the music shop. It was something to do, she told herself. Of course, she hadn't seen him around. If she had, she wouldn't have known what to do.

As she repeated her journey, she passed four or five junctions and fancied she saw the vagrant from the morning. He was round the corner of Griffton Boulevard, the road that ran along the beach.

She ducked out of sight for a moment around a lamppost. At least, she thought it had been him. It was the same build and gait. She was on the corner of Goblin Valley Road. It wasn't that far from the public library. If she went there, at least she would be in a public place if he decided to make a nuisance of himself again with his crazy talk. Not that anyone intervened these days. There was a case on the news the other day about a group of hooded yobs rampaging on the trains around Griffton. Nobody lifted a finger.

SHE PASSED DEADWOOD AND DRIFTWOOD, Broad Path, and Pomeroy Avenue. The tramp was following at a distance. Roasting Vale Lane wound up through the old manufacturing yards and up past the new businesses, the web designers, and business consultancies.

She applied for work experience with some firms there last year but didn't get a place. She crossed Falcon and Phoenix, Stony Bridge, and Pebble Road and finally approached the library, glancing over her shoulder.

At last, the tramp had dropped out of sight.

12345

LAKE MISSED Rachel by a few minutes. She had gone wandering off on her lunch break, the other girl said. He spent a couple of minutes checking out some CDs so as not to appear rude or over-keen and then headed out again. If he'd had his rollerblades with him, he would have eaten up the journey between the office and the record shop.

"Oh well, that's life," he thought.

GRIFFTON LIBRARY WAS a huge square building with a couple of round satellite hubs connected to it by long corridor tendrils. The main body of the building rose four storeys, and Rachel found herself on the third floor, looking at the fiction. She had read a great page-turner a few months back by Joshua Raven and wanted to read the sequel.

The arrangement of the windows and shelves cast long shadows into the corners of the room where a small number of lone readers floated and browsed or stood statue still, staring at the spines.

Thinking about the strange man in Rock and Shock and what a lucky escape she had had, Rachel walked over to the R section near the top of the staircase. The fiction section of the Griffton Library was impressive.

"Rackley, Rat, Ravelli, Raven," she mouthed, following the progression of letters down the rack. Eventually, she found her book on the bottom shelf, at the end of a row. She crouched to pluck her prize, holding the metal frame to steady herself. As she stood up again, she almost toppled into the long-haired tramp who was standing at her shoulder.

He grinned through blackened teeth and put his finger to his lips, grabbing her arm.

Rachel screamed for all she was worth, but his huge hand had already smothered her mouth.

CHAPTER 10

"Don't make a noise," hissed the man. "Stay silent, and I'll take my hand away."

Rachel's eyes flashed around. She nodded immediately just to get his stinking hand off her face.

The stench of the man grated the back of her throat. It was like a paste of garlic and urine, mashed up and slathered across her tonsils. She kept telling herself she was in a public place. Any minute, someone would come and demand to know what was going on. But then she also knew about the many times when members of the public just stood around and watched, like on the trains or in the streets after dark.

"What would Mum do?" she asked herself. "What would she do in this situation?"

Rachel had no idea at all.

After lunch, Lake Emerson found himself back at the Griffton Library. He planned to continue his research into the local shipping company that was treating their staff badly.

One of the great things about working on a paper was that

he could legitimately be anywhere in town. He could be at the library, or perhaps a café asking someone questions, or maybe at someone's offices following up a lead. He felt like a real reporter, except that he wasn't allowed to write anything much. But being the junior he was, the editor rarely grilled him about his day.

Most research is done on the internet these days because pretty much everything is up there somewhere. If it isn't, there's always LexisNexis or some other news-searching tool. But Lake needed local shipping records, and these were not online yet.

He paused as he entered the broad lobby of the library and glanced at the massive double staircase at the centre back of the hall. His eyes followed the sweep of the hardwood banisters right until they disappeared out of sight. He thought he had heard a noise that sounded like a mouse squeaking.

Then he shrugged and ducked down towards the sub-basement of the library through an archway to the left.

He wanted to hunt down some handwritten notes on an obscure shipping record that probably didn't exist. Two sets of staircases led the way. Then, he had to go down an echoing corridor and into a well-lit reading area surrounded by floor-to-ceiling shelving. The papers muffled any sound from above.

Soon, Lake fell into a pattern of thumbing through rack after rack of public documents. The search could take some time, he thought, wishing he'd brought a flask of coffee with him.

THE SCARY MAN indicated he wanted Rachel to walk toward the back of the library, where the wide elevator was. To get there, they had to pass several high bookshelves packed full of novels. There were a few people reading the books, but most of them minded their own business. One or two gave the man a quick glance, but something in his expression clearly made them turn away quickly. Perhaps it was the insane grin and staring eyes.

Rachel and the man walked close together with her in front, his hand prodding her back every so often.

Then, they were at the back of the library. The man called the lift. They were on floor three, and the lift was not in a hurry.

After what seemed like an age, the lift came with much huffing and puffing. Hustling her quickly into the wide lift, he punched the button for the ground floor. They watched the doors closing slowly. Rachel was tucked away at the back of the lift, trying not to throw up.

From deep within the folds of the tramp's clothing, he fetched out a cell phone and called a number.

"I have the girl. What does he want me to do? Make sure you let him know I will do whatever I have to. For him."

12345

DANIEL HARCOURT WAS SITTING in his brown leather chair behind a pristine desk. As usual, he had several large-scale computer infrastructure projects on the go for some of the biggest corporations in the business. Not that his desk betrayed this fact. He leaned back, stared out of the window overlooking the sea, and carried on talking quietly into his mobile phone.

"Samyaza only said he wanted to give her a scare, not kill her, you idiot," Daniel hissed.

He sighed and rolled his eyes, listening to the man's excuses.

"I don't care," he spat. "Let her go. She has a job to do. Just stick to the plan."

12345

RACHEL STARED as the man dropped his cell phone into his pocket and grimaced to himself.

He pulled a face before mimicking in a horrible voice, "Samyaza says: I have your finger. That means I own you. Await your orders, which you will get soon, or you lose another finger. Or maybe the whole hand."

He grinned, showing his blackened teeth.

"And remember, we can get to you anywhere," he growled.

As the lift approached the ground floor, he hit the button for the lowest level, the sub-basement.

"Stay here," he warned, waving one finger. Then he departed.

Rachel cowered in the recesses of the lift, watching the doors close behind the man.

WHEN THE LIFT opened at the sub-basement level, Lake immediately saw Rachel sitting on the floor at the back.

He had heard the lift coming, but as soon as it opened and he'd glanced up, he was out of his seat, casting aside the papers he'd pulled out.

"Rachel?" he said. "What are you…? Are you okay?"

He helped her to her feet, and she all but bolted into the room with him.

For quite a while, she just sat and cried. He couldn't get a word out of her, but she seemed glad he was there.

WHEN THE LIFT opened at the sub-basement level, Lake immediately saw Rachel sitting on the floor at the back.

AS THEY SAT CLOSE TOGETHER, Rachel began to tell Lake about the man. Not everything, but about how he came into the shop and then followed her to the library.

"We must call the police," he decided, swiftly finding his phone. He was pleased to see he could get a signal down in the sub-basement. But before he could punch the numbers in, Rachel whispered, "No."

"At least we can get them to look out for this man," Lake reasoned.

"No. He let me go. There's nothing to tell." Rachel stared into space, hugging her body with her arms.

Lake tried to put his arms around her but thought better of it. "Don't you want him caught? What if he tries it on with someone else? We have to do something."

"Could you call Iona for me and tell her what happened? She's my friend who I work with."

"Of course. Let's go up," commanded Lake. "I don't reckon he'll still be hanging around."

"Would you call her from here?" asked Rachel.

Lake paused. "Okay," he conceded softly. He stood up. "And don't leave me," pleaded Rachel.

"Okay," he repeated and sat down again.

While Lake made the call, she wrestled with whether or not to tell him what the man had said: the threats he'd made at the end. She looked around the records room and was glad they had it to themselves. The place was cosy and warm, and she felt safe. Even so, she eyed the lift a couple of times just to be sure.

If they could get to her anywhere, that could mean they were watching her right now, she thought. If they were watching her, then there could be several of them, and maybe not just the dirty man and the man on the phone, she reasoned. But why her, and what did they want with her? She was a sixteen-year-old girl, for goodness' sake.

"There was something else," she informed Lake when he was off the phone.

"The man said he knew who took my finger. Which means it was cut off by someone. It wasn't eaten by a panther or a bird."

Lake raised his eyebrows and muttered, "A bird?"

Rachel carried on, "It wasn't my dad at all. He had nothing to do with this."

She had known this in her head, and now she knew in her heart that he was innocent. Walls began to come down. She suddenly wanted to see her father.

"Hold on a bit – you're telling me you know who did that to you?" asked Lake.

"That's what I said. It's someone called Samyaza something. Or just Samyaza."

"Sounds like the Yakuza."

"Who are they?"

"The Japanese mafia. They cut people's fingers off, too. Maybe it's them?"

"What on earth do the Japanese mafia want with me? I've never even been to Japan, let alone met any Japanese people. At least, I don't think I have."

Lake leapt up and went over to the bank of computer terminals. He plonked himself down in a seat and started tapping at the keyboard.

"Here we go. Yakuza. They've got a ritual called Yubitsume, or finger-cutting, which they use as a form of penance or apology, it says here. You're not squeamish, are you?"

"After what I've been through, what do you think?"

"Guess not. Okay, it says, 'Upon a first offense, the transgressor must cut off the tip of his left pinky finger and hand the severed portion to his boss.' It comes from the traditional way of holding a Japanese sword. 'The bottom three fingers of each hand are used to grip the sword tightly, with the thumb and index fingers slightly loose. The removal of digits starting with the little finger moving up the hand to the index finger progressively weakens a person's sword grip.'"

"Okay, stop talking," snapped Rachel. She put her fingers to her lips, her face pale.

Lake read on silently.

After a long while, Rachel stated, "I'm not convinced of this. Granted, it's my left hand and the little finger, but I'm sure the man said 'Samyaza,' not 'Yakuza.'"

"Not a name I've heard," said Lake.

"Do the search anyway," implored Rachel.

"Here we go. Samyaza. Says here: 'Samyaza, also known as

Shemyazaz, Semjaza, Shemyaza, Shemhazai, and Amezarak, believe it or not, is a fallen angel – a demon – of Hebrew and Christian tradition. He ranked in the heavenly hierarchy as one of the Grigori – meaning 'Watchers' in Greek.'" Lake grinned to himself. "You've got to love the web."

"A demon? A demon's got my finger?" screeched Rachel, clearly horrified.

Lake waved his hand in the air and murmured, "I'm sure it's just some kook jumping on the name. Makes a great story, doesn't it? Wait, there's more. Apparently, the name 'Shemyazaz' means 'infamous rebellion.' Looks like this guy and his cronies apparently fell from heaven to earth and ran after human women. Then they had children called The Nephilim, and get this, these are giants – half angel, half human. And guess what? These Nephilim, or 'fallen ones,' also eat people. Can you believe this stuff? What a load of old rubbish."

Rachel was silent.

"There's more that I haven't told you," she said, her face gaunt and pale. "That night, after you came to see me at the hospital, something really strange happened."

❧ 12345 ❧

THEY SPENT the afternoon together in the library, Lake and Rachel. After Rachel had told Lake about the panther, she was sure he would want nothing to do with her ever again.

He accompanied her home on the bus, more out of duty than anything else, thought Rachel, and then he went on his way. "So much for that," thought Rachel.

Iona had wanted to tell the police about the man who had assaulted Rachel. Ben gave Rachel the rest of the day off but decided that now was the time to get CCTV installed in the shop, wired to his office in the back. He'd get it sorted on Monday.

"It's not just you, sweetie," whispered Iona on the phone that evening. "He might come back for me."

"If he does, then that's the time to call the police," insisted Rachel.

"I don't get it. The guy assaulted you. He's on the loose."

"There's nothing to get. I just don't think the police can, like, do anything. He didn't hurt me…"

"But he could have."

"But he didn't."

"But he might go after you again. Or someone else," shrieked Iona, her swirly voice climbing higher and higher.

"Yeah, he might," acknowledged Rachel.

HER FATHER WASN'T AROUND at home, which was nothing new. Rachel eventually climbed up to bed with the events of the day crowding her mind. If she really was being stalked by the forces of darkness and evil, then what chance did she have?

An uncomfortable sleep carried her away late at night. She dreamed of a rotating vortex made of dust and lights. It started off on the horizon, looking like a sea storm far out at sea. It eventually approached the city of Griffton, which lay in a valley with an escarpment to the north and water to the south.

The vortex of cloudy dust settled over the city and immediately flooded her brain, showering her with weird static. Translucent tendrils of dust flowed and twisted, and in the midst of them were set the most beautiful lights. They were like tiny angels, emanating their own individual glow in colours far beyond the rainbow shades that were familiar to her.

The dust started to choke her, pulling at her throat and trying to suffocate her. But all the while, she gazed ahead, enthralled by the spectral lights, dancing and winking and drawing her with their preternatural radiance.

Her eyes began to glow under their lids.

CHAPTER 11

The day after was Sunday, a day of fear and shadows. Rachel woke up in a cold sweat at 42 Russet Road, on the east side of Griffton. She felt like she had been drugged. Her limbs felt heavy. Her nerves were jangling. The stump of her finger ached. That was where her left little finger had been taken by Samyaza, she thought. A shiver passed from her shoulders to her legs.

Looking up in bed, she imagined she saw a creature in the corner, crouching near the door. She stared at it for a long time as she went through the process of waking up. It could have been a long-winged dark angel hiding in the shadow cast by the dim light from the window and a chair.

"Go away," she quaked.

Eventually, she summoned all her courage and went to have a look, which meant getting out of bed.

Further examination found no such creature.

"The mind can play tricks on you," she thought. She checked out the shadow again, just to be sure. The creature was back. Next, it was just a shadow again.

She blinked, sitting on the bed.

She wasn't hungry for food. So, she had a glass of cold milk for breakfast instead, which didn't make her feel any better. What was more, her father was being uncommunicative and evasive. He made some excuses and left the house mid-morning. He would not be back that day.

Iona was on the phone again, being annoying. She was whining about how they should have got the police involved. Rachel felt irritable. She snapped at her friend, perhaps for the first time since she had known her. She hated herself for it because Iona was such a 'peace and love' kind of girl. It was a bit like swatting a butterfly.

The person she really wanted to talk to was Lake Emerson. She wanted him to call her and check she was all right. But he hadn't. He had probably formed the strong impression she was a complete nutcase. Mind you, it was still Sunday morning, and there was still time for him to call before she wrote him off. He was cute, though. He was a skater and a writer: her type of guy. But she wished he'd just call her.

Meanwhile, the dream about the vortex swirled around in her head. She could feel the presence of the lights in the cloud wooing her.

"I am going mad," she said out loud.

❧ 12345 ❧

BY THE AFTERNOON, Rachel was restless and bored. There was nothing on television, and she was done with movies. She wasn't interested in her playlists and didn't want to connect with anyone online.

"Useless," she grunted as she turned off the screen after hopping through the Freeview channels. There were a thousand channels, but there was nothing on. She threw down the remote.

The telephone rang.

"Rach, it's me," chimed the familiar voice. It was Lara. "Oh, hi, Lara," replied Rachel.

Lara was friendly. "How's Racoon?"

"I'm good. You?"

"Still packing, but we're almost good to go, as they say in LA!"

"When are you leaving?"

"I've already told you a million times. It's Wednesday week."

"Wednesday after next?" groaned Rachel, wincing. Where on earth had the time gone? The end of the term seemed like just the other day. She was conscious of the growing distance between the supposed best friends. Each day widened the gulf between them as more and more weird stuff happened: the Samyaza stuff, the dreams, the emotions. There was too much to communicate to Lara, who was leaving her anyway.

"We're getting together tonight. If you're not too busy," continued Lara.

"The Pirate's Paradise?"

Lara shot back, "Where else? The gang's going to be there. Oh, and my brother and his friend Lake. I know you like him. Lake, that is."

"I never said…"

"Oh, you guys are so obvious. It's written all over you," Lara sounded like she was smirking. "Later then?"

"Later."

12345

THEY MET at the usual time, around seven thirty, at the Pirate's Paradise, their cosy local pub, which smelled strongly of beer and crisps. The usual crowd was there: Lara and Suzanne, Harry and Carina, and the rest.

Joel, Lara's older brother, who was eighteen, was also there, cracking gags and keeping everyone amused. However, Lake hadn't come out tonight, and Rachel was sad.

Did it mean he didn't like her anymore? Had their conversation yesterday been too much for him? Then she told herself not to be so silly. He was probably away for the day. Knowing him, he had probably gone out rollerblading in the morning and stayed out all day. She knew he liked doing that and being free.

They sat in their usual booth around a wooden table marked with rings from the glasses, and Lara sank ginger ales and laughed too much, Rachel thought. Oh, well, she's going soon, mused Rachel. Things are going to change again.

Later on, she got to catch up with Lara. They had broken out of the communal conversation and carved out a private chat on the side.

"It's not going to be easy leaving all my friends. I love you and the guys. I've known everyone for, like, a million years. All my life, pretty much," complained Lara. "I am going to miss you, Racoon," she added.

"Oh, Lemur. We've been friends forever. You know it. But I know you have to move on. I also know you'll miss the gang. But you're going to love it out there. Where is it you're going?" Rachel smiled.

"Oh, shut up, Racoon, you loon."

"So, anyway. How's the packing going? Got any of my stuff you feel the need to give back?"

"I've got a special box, and it's filled with stuff. Some of it's yours, and some of it's our stuff. Like that photo book we did last summer – remember? And the tapes we did trying to be rapper girls."

"You don't still have that! How old are those tapes? I mean, it was old tech when your dad gave us the recorder."

"And then there's the dress. We ended up with one each, and you still kept borrowing mine, so I've finally given it to you," nodded Lara.

"Oh, thanks. But listen to us – you're not going yet. Are you? I mean, you're still around for a bit longer."

"A week and a half."

"Yeah, a bit longer," smiled Rachel.

Someone else wanted Lara's attention, so Rachel took the

opportunity to look away and wipe her eyes. The bar was getting busy now, even for a Sunday. It was gone eight-thirty.

She saw her favourite barman, Steve, who smiled at her and wiped the bar, and her least favourite barman, the sly one, who was busy with a customer.

Rachel decided to go to the ladies and made her excuses. She was feeling tired, and the emotional strain of the parting was starting to take its toll.

The toilets were empty and smelled of lemons. While she was in the cubicle, she heard someone enter the ladies. The person pushed a note under the door. Rachel looked down and saw the paper.

"Who is it?" she called. "Lara?"

No answer. The door of the toilets closed hard. She waited for a few seconds, holding her breath. The words of the tramp came back to her. Remember, we can get to you anywhere, he had said. Anywhere is anywhere: her bedroom, a hospital bed, or the public toilets of a rock and roll pub above Griffton Beach.

With a shaking hand, she reached down and grabbed the paper that had been pushed under her door. She unfolded it and saw a message and a tiny picture of a hand with the little finger missing. The message was written in an old-style typeface.

"First assignment: Go to Griffton Cliff immediately. Take the next bus to Lower Ledge Crossing. Don't tell a soul."

❦ 12345 ❦

RACHEL QUICKLY LEFT THE LADIES' toilets. She briefly visited the table where her friends were sitting. Lara was looking at her strangely.

Rachel said hastily, "Lara, I have to go."

"But Rachel…where?" implored Lara. "It's still early." Lara peered at her watch to make sure. Her friends gave her puzzled looks. But in a fog, Rachel just stared at them.

Then she left.

"Rach, you okay? You're being so weird," called Lara after her as Rachel walked quickly towards the door.

"I have to go," Rachel found herself muttering. The noise of the pub receded.

Outside, it was cool. She could see the activity of the pub through the windows and knew she was now utterly alone.

She made her way to the bus stop, which was just along from the pub and towards the beach. She saw the waves leaping far out at sea. The air above the water was very calm, and there was an absence of birds. They usually went diving into the sea and soaring into the sky. All was calm; too calm.

"There can't be any buses at this time," she thought. Then she took out the note and glanced at it again. She saw it meant business.

She stood and looked at the bus timetable, noticing that the buses ran until nine o'clock. That was the last bus, and the hour was fast approaching. How she would get home after 'the assignment' was anyone's guess.

"Maybe they'll just murder me out there on Griffton Cliff," she thought.

12345

Daniel was in the study of his Griffton mansion. His wife, Arabella, was out with a friend, and his children were asleep in bed in another part of the house.

He paced up and down between his bookshelves and his hardwood desk and clenched his fists. He was wrestling with Samyaza, and not for the first time.

"I've done what you asked me to do. I've done it all. Can't you let her go now? She's just a child."

He knew Samyaza was there but remained silent, which infuriated him.

"I came looking for you. That was my mistake. But she, she has no idea what you're capable of."

Suddenly, Samyaza appeared in his mind's eye. It was the horribly familiar form of the demon, disfigured and bent over.

"So, you would trade your son Rory for the girl?" asked Samyaza.

"What do you mean? You leave Rory out of this. He's innocent. He has nothing to do with you."

"You're forgetting how it works, Daniel. You work for me. I own you. I own your family."

Daniel blanched. Samyaza had been back in his life for a matter of weeks, and he was already back to his old tricks of blackmailing him about his family. Of course, Daniel had heard it all before, but it didn't make it any less difficult.

"Once again, would you put your son up as a one-for-one trade for the girl? You give Rory up to me, and the girl goes free?"

"You know, I would never do that."

"I didn't think so. I was just messing about," sneered Samyaza.

"I hate you, Samyaza. I always have."

"Not always, surely? We had fun together, didn't we? In the beginning."

"You go to hell," spat Daniel. "That's my boy."

12345

In seconds, a familiar green Griffton bus came from downtown and stopped next to her at the bus stop. It was empty except for the driver. Shivering slightly, she climbed aboard and paid the fare up to Lower Ledge Crossing on Griffton Cliff. The door closed, and the bus took her away.

She stared hard at the driver as she shuffled past him and continued to stare as she found her seat at the back of the bus. She didn't want anyone sitting behind her. She wanted to get a good look at the driver and anyone who might come aboard between now and the cliff.

As the bus moved away, Rachel slumped into a daze. She was terrified at what waited for her at Griffton Cliff. Of course, she thought frequently about running from her assignment, but where would she go? If she went home, they would find her. If she left town, they would find her. She was trapped.

She closed her eyes and rocked herself.

12345

THE JOURNEY SEEMED INCREDIBLY LONG. During the hour and a half it took to traverse the city and climb the base of the cliffs, nighttime closed in, and the skies darkened.

Rachel sailed past many familiar sights. She passed shops she'd visited, the college, the library, houses of friends, and houses of acquaintances.

All the while, she thought of escaping. Perhaps now was the time to tell the police about everything. But then, what could they do against an enemy with many faces – and no face? Fear locked her onto the route she was on.

She looked at the back of the driver's head and knew he couldn't help her now, assuming he was neutral in all this.

No one could help her.

12345

LOWER LEDGE CROSSING was the end of the line. It was the last stop just before the cliffs started to get really steep, and thick undergrowth took over from the manmade roads and paths.

Rachel had been up here a few times to see the views over Griffton and the sea and chatter with Lara and the gang. The truth was there wasn't much up here of interest apart from the view. They'd done a little bit of exploring and knew some of the terrain very well. But it was really only limited to a couple of paths that led up to a vantage point over the city.

Rachel had no idea why she was required here.

The bus driver let her out at Lower Ledge Crossing and did his usual turnaround before pressing the gas and rumbling back down the road. Rachel was left in the middle of nowhere. From where she stood, her view of the city was obscured by a row of bushes that lined the top of the road. There was still a small amount of light from the evening sky. In addition, the city threw up an orange-yellow glow from its buildings and streetlights. She could make out the paths that she and Lara knew and wondered whether she was meant to walk up the cliff that way.

She fished out the note yet again and turned it over, looking for more instructions, but all it said was: "First assignment: Go to Griffton Cliff immediately. Take the next bus to Lower Ledge Crossing. Don't tell a soul."

"Am I just meant to stand here?" she asked no one in particular. Perhaps they were waiting for her in the shadows of the trees.

She waited and listened. All she could hear was the sound of the wind carried from the ocean across the roofs of the city and up to Griffton Cliff.

Then she saw the lights.

CHAPTER 12

Some people might describe them as UFOs, unidentified flying objects. Other people might have said they were just fireflies. A child might say it was Tinkerbell and her fairy friends.

Rachel watched the dancing lights that hung above the path with her mouth open. They were stunningly beautiful. There also seemed to be some intelligence in there. First of all, there had been one white light with a fuzzy halo around it. It bounced up and down in the air and almost touched the path in its downstroke. Then, another appeared further up the path.

They played a game of tag, swapping places at a leisurely pace. Rachel had whispered a greeting in awe of the lights. She did not get any sense that they were sinister and quickly understood that they wanted her to follow them. She looked around her and swiftly worked out that there was no point in staying where she was. There was also no point in going along with the lights, she reasoned, but did she have a choice?

When the third leaping light appeared, she was ready to throw caution to the wind and follow the lights wherever they led her. The three lights played an interesting game of bouncing on top of each other as they moved down the path. Rachel went after them, taking each step steadily and slowly. They inched up the path that she knew, which ascended to the place overlooking the city. The bouncing lights lit enough of the way for her to see where they were going. She could see enough to avoid the sticks and jutting rocks.

When they reached the spot, the lights indicated they wanted Rachel to continue walking. She couldn't see where they were meant to go because it looked like they were hemmed in on all sides by thick, green growth.

But the lights lined up and combined their brightness to show Rachel a small gap between the bushes.

"Where are you taking me? I don't want to go any further." She trembled, starting to feel scared again.

She felt foolish enough that she was following a set of moving lights. But now she was talking to them, which was obviously proof she had gone insane. Regardless, the realisation came to her that these lights, the panther, the tramp, and Samyaza, did not have her best interests at heart. It was time to take a stand, literally.

"I'm going to stay here," blurted Rachel. She planted her feet in the soil and folded her arms, feeling brave. After all, what could a bunch of small lights do to her?

Then she watched the lights as they disappeared through the gap in the bushes. Rachel raised her eyebrows.

As they went, they left a profound darkness behind them.

FOR A WHILE, Rachel stood and watched the place where they had been. Then she turned to look across the valley. It was very peaceful up here, with the breeze blowing and the hiss and roar of the sea in the distance. She smelled the salty air that was so familiar to her. She watched as the city prepared for nighttime down below.

Some lights were going off, and others were switching on.

Cars drove around with their headlights on full beam. The distance made Griffton look pocket-sized. The lights in the valley were reminiscent of the tiny bouncing lights that had led her to this spot.

She turned on her heel and picked her way through the gap in the bushes in pursuit of the bouncing lights.

The lights led her on a long hike. First, they led her through some spiky undergrowth, then up a hill, then down a little, along a winding path, and out into the open again.

She found herself at the edge of the cliff again, overlooking Griffton from even higher up. She stood on a thin ledge, facing the elements, with thick trees hemming her in. The wind whistled through her hair. The valley lay in darkness now, although there was still enough light to make out major buildings, parks, and the map of vein-like streets.

The three bright lights had disappeared over the edge of the cliff. The hair on the back of Rachel's neck bristled as she waited.

"Assignment, assignment. This is my first assignment. What does that mean? And why aren't I allowed to tell anyone? 'Don't tell a soul,' the note says," Rachel mused.

Suddenly, a thought struck her. They were going to push her off Griffton Cliff. They had brought her out here so she could plunge to her death, and no one would know about it. They would find her body at the base of the cliff, another of Griffton's rare suicide cases. It would be a clean, open-and-shut case.

She stepped back from the edge and squeezed her eyes shut. But she had the note. That would prove it wasn't suicide because it had instructions for her to come up here. And why was she thinking about suicide, anyway? Surely, if they wanted her dead, they would have killed her in her bed on day one.

In the distance, from the east and the west, two of the bright lights came hurtling towards the cliff. The third light also approached quickly from lower down. She watched as they raced towards each other, marking streaks of lightning in the air. It was thrilling. The tiny lights were playing at being the Red Arrows.

Then they collided, exploding together in a cloud of sparks.

They seemed to multiply before her eyes. There were more bright lights flying around with their fuzzy halos. They were beautiful. A thick cloud of dust had arisen after the lights had collided, like the mushroom cloud above an atomic bomb. The smoky fog spread outwards, radiating in all directions from the epicentre of the explosion.

Inside the grey cloud, all the tiny lights were flying around, dancing, sparkling, and entertaining her.

Within seconds, the cloud had filled the space between the explosion and the point at which she stood. Then, a wave of fog washed over her, hitting her with a narcotic rush. Colours swirled, sounds blared, and she closed her eyes.

She then had what she could only describe as some sort of crazy dream.

The details of the dream would always remain obscure to her. But, looking back on it, what she did remember was her mother's face, smiling kindly at her. It filled the whole of her mind, and she felt such love. It was amazing.

This vivid part of the dream transformed into a normal dream that went on through the night. All that was left of it in the morning were light impressions of storm clouds and motion.

Rachel awoke to feel cold water lapping at her feet. She felt it rolling towards her and slipping away again.

She opened her eyes and stared at the morning sky. Rachel screamed.

Then she propped herself up on one elbow and found herself lying on Griffton beach, with her toes in the morning tide. She looked across the rippling white surface of the water and saw the sun rising.

Rachel screamed again.

"No one is going to believe this," murmured Rachel to herself, not for the first time that morning.

She pulled her cardigan around herself and sipped the cup of tea she had bought from the tiny beachside café called Ramshack Café. Griffton was waking up some hours after she had watched it fall asleep. She stared out of the window and daydreamed about the dancing lights. She was still thinking about her mother and how much she missed her. Not a day went by when she didn't. Though she had slept, she was completely exhausted.

Rachel sniffed. Not surprisingly, she had caught a cold somewhere between falling asleep on the cliff and waking up on the beach.

She also realised somewhere along the way she had lost her phone. Where it lay was anyone's guess.

"No one is going to believe this. Not even I believe this," muttered Rachel. The waitress, Maureen, who was known as Mo, smiled at her from over the other side of the café. Rachel knew her from her many visits to Ramshack Café over the years, sometimes with her friends, but mostly alone.

"Fancy some breakfast?" called Mo.

"Why not?" replied Rachel. "I'll have some toast and jam. Please."

☙ 12345 ❧

Lake Emerson had been working feverishly since he had seen Rachel. He had amassed a whole folder of documents, which he had carefully labelled and stuffed into a brown envelope.

He knew Rachel didn't have a decent computer or phone, which was really unusual these days. So, printouts were his best option for getting this great information to her.

What he had discovered was dynamite in story terms. It eclipsed anything he had worked on so far, particularly the shipping story. That was a small fry compared to this. It was a 'Nib'

– 'news in brief' – compared with a front-page lead story plus inside features.

The meeting in the library had been eye-opening for him, mind-blowing even. Not only was Rachel Race an exquisite creature, a real treasure, but she also did more for him than any other girl had done. She intrigued him.

The stuff she had told him had at first amused him, then interested him, and finally intrigued him. You couldn't really argue with the finger thing, which was mysterious in itself, to say the least. He had always reckoned it was the father who did it but was willing to concede that maybe it wasn't.

Then there was the panther thing in the hospital. That was also pretty mysterious. But the clincher was the tramp. Granted, he hadn't seen the man, or the panther, come to mention it, but he did, in fact, believe Rachel. Even though she was probably a fruitcake. A cute fruitcake.

As he started to research Samyaza and what he was all about, he had unearthed some really fascinating things.

By Monday morning, he was ready to rollerblade around to Rachel's house and post the envelope through her door on his way to work. He strapped on his blades, checked his hair in the mirror, and left the house.

❧ 12345 ❧

RACHEL PAID for her breakfast at Ramshack Café, the small diner on the beach, and tried to smile at Mo.

She attempted conversation but instantly regretted it. "How's business?" she asked.

"You're my first customer," retorted Mo. "So I am," acknowledged Rachel.

She took her change as the handset on the counter rang. Mo took the call, looked blank for a moment while she listened, and then commented, "You're Rachel Race, right?"

"That's me," she answered, stony-faced. "Then, it's for you."

Rachel squinted out of the windows, trying to see who was spying on her. Seeing no one, she took the receiver. Mo walked away.

"Who is this?" she demanded.

An androgynous voice at the other end of the line informed in a bored voice, "Your second assignment is to go to Lupus Street Chemist in Sandy Bottom Cove at six o'clock this evening. Take the bag on the counter. Do not open it. Keep hold of it until you hear from us. Follow these orders or lose another finger. Remember, don't tell a soul."

The speaker hung up.

TODAY WAS MONDAY, Rachel's day off. She worked on Saturdays, Tuesdays, and Wednesdays. The phone call had cut short her leisurely breakfasting, and Rachel was starting to feel like her life was no longer her own.

Lupus Street Chemist was not a pharmacy she had heard of. She was, however, familiar with the name Sandy Bottom Cove, knowing it as a small village further along the coast. She'd never been there, but her father had mentioned it a few times, and he'd picked up some work from there at one point. Also, it was a very long bus ride to get there. The train might stop somewhere near the village, but Rachel wasn't sure.

"Well, I haven't really got a choice," thought Rachel. She grabbed her cardigan and went looking for a bus.

FORTY-FIVE MINUTES LATER, she was at her front door. She had decided that she was going to have a shower and get clean, threats or no threats. What was the worst they could do to her? She wasn't a huge fan of sleeping in her clothes, though she'd been to more than one party where she'd ended up doing that.

As she opened the front door, the package Lake had left her got pushed away and wedged under a rug. Unknowingly, Rachel skipped past it.

Noticing her father was out at work, Rachel started to fly up the steps. She paused a few steps from the bottom to look around the front room and peer across into the kitchen. Nothing was out of place. Up in her room, she observed every-thing was as it had been.

In the shower, she had time to reflect on what was going on.

Although she hated being manipulated in this way, those lights had been beautiful, and seeing her mother so clearly, as though she was really there, had been an experience beyond words.

When she thought about it, this secret mission had an exciting side to it. She was being forced to travel to strange places and face who knows what sorts of dangers. The first assignment hadn't been too bad. It had been a real adventure, with lots of surprises, and had not actually been harmful.

Now, they wanted her to pick up some sort of package, which could be anything. It wasn't such a big deal. It was just one big magical mystery tour. The less she knew, the better. The prospect thrilled her.

Then she caught herself and was appalled. These people had taken her finger, and that was plainly unacceptable.

Lake Emerson had been trying to call Rachel all morning to see if she had received his envelope. Her phone just kept going to voicemail. Eventually, distracted beyond belief, he decided to take an early lunch and pop around to see her. He had skated from the Griffton News offices all the way to her house and knocked at the door.

There was no answer. He tried knocking again and calling

out. Finally, he gave up and decided to pop back to his house to grab some food.

BACK AT HOME, he fixed himself a peanut butter sandwich and grabbed a pack of salt and vinegar crisps and an apple. He went through to the front room with his plate to eat his lunch in front of the news.

As he sat down, he believed he heard a noise upstairs. "Mum?" he called out. "Dad?"

Either one of them could have come home early from work or have nipped home, like him, to have lunch. That was because they both worked locally, and their journey back was no longer than fifteen minutes.

There was no reply from upstairs. He left his plate on the floor and went quietly upstairs. If it was a burglar, he wanted to catch him red-handed. If it was a cat, then stealth was also the order of the day, thought Lake.

He saw a cloud of smoke at the top of the stairs. "Something's burning," he thought.

As he climbed the stairs, he noticed something strange about the smoke. It didn't behave like the sort of smoke that came from burning furniture. This was a thin grey mist that seemed to have spots of light in it. They looked like white, winking Christmas lights. "How very strange," he thought.

As he ascended, he found himself in the thick of the swirling mists. The lights entranced him, dancing around his head like tiny fireflies or fairies. He smiled and watched them buzzing around. The cloud itself seemed to be alive. Lake reached the top of the stairs and walked deeper into the mist.

CHAPTER 13

It was just after noon, so Rachel had plenty of time to get to the chemist in Sandy Bottom Cove. "If that was all these people wanted her to do, then it was a pretty easy gig," she convinced herself. She just had to go over there and pick up some drugs or whatever.

She resolved to figure out a way to get out of this blackmail situation as soon as she could. It would be great if only she could shake off the tiredness. She had a constant fuzzy feeling in her head. If she could do that, she might be able to think straight.

She was putting together a bag of things, throwing them onto her bed as she thought of them. There was her book, a bottle of water, a banana, a chocolate bar, her money, and some chewing gum, just in case. But she felt nervous about going out without a mobile phone.

Rachel made a quick call to the train station from the land-line. The station was within walking distance from the house. She discovered the destination was an hour away by train. The train went along the coast. It was the best option. It stopped at every little village station from Griffton City to Sandy Bottom, but the bus service was even worse. The buses were slower and stopped at every little stop from here to Sandy Bottom Cove.

Taxis were out of the question because the trip would be far too expensive. Rachel didn't drive or have access to a car, so that was out.

She decided to leave at four, so she had plenty of time. The four-thirty train would get in at around half-five, leaving loads of time to find Lupus Street Chemist. How hard could it be to find a chemist in a village? She was fairly sure Sandy Bottom Cove was a small place.

LARA WAS HANGING out with Suzanne in the mall in central Griffton, sitting on tall bar stools and nibbling at their double chocolate ice creams.

"She was acting really strangely," complained Lara for the umpteenth time.

Suzanne rolled her eyes, also for the umpteenth time. It was what she did best. It only encouraged Lara.

"I mean, she's obviously not coping with me moving to California," moaned Lara.

"Jealous," replied Suzanne, nodding. "Definitely jealous."

"You think so? You think she's jealous?"

"Well, take me for example. I am," smiled Suzanne. "Jealous, that is. All that sunshine. All those shops. Then you'll meet a surfer boy – a real surfer boy, not like the ones round here."

Lara laughed. Around them, other young people window-shopped, wandering around and chatting. Young mums dressed in tracksuits and full makeup pushed their babies around and looked bored.

"Do you reckon she's always been like this, but I just haven't noticed?" asked Lara.

"Rachel? Definitely. I think – number one, she's jealous of you, and number two, she's a mad cow. Poor dear. She's her own worst enemy."

"This is my best friend we're talking about. I can't believe I'm talking about Rachel like this."

"Listen, Lara. If you want my opinion, she should be here hanging out with us. In a week, you're not going to be around. Instead, she goes off like some drama queen, and no one can get hold of her because she's in this massive mood."

"She's always been a bit moody," Lara reflected. Then she sighed, "I have tried calling her."

"Well, that's my opinion, for what it's worth."

"Right, thanks," commented Lara. She stared across the mall, watching the escalators going round and round.

⚜ 1₂₃₄₅ ⚜

SITTING on the train to Sandy Bottom Cove, Rachel started to have a complete panic. Here she was, a small girl on a big train in a big city, with no idea where she was going. She had nothing to defend herself with if she got into danger. Then there was this mystery chemist. She would be too far from help and without a mobile phone if trouble was waiting for her there.

Come to think of it, she didn't even have her coat if it got cold or rained. Then, if her purse got stolen, she'd be totally stuck. There were so many things to worry about and plenty of time to worry about them.

A gang of kids were rioting at the end of her carriage. She tried to ignore them. But soon, one of them ripped off the seat. He managed to pull up the whole unit with his bare hands and cast it aside. Rachel glimpsed the tattoo on his left upper arm.

These were Zodiacs, Griffton's particular brand of gang culture.

Boys who joined the Zodiacs tended to be out of work, disaffected, and prone to violence. Invariably, they shared squats together or lived at home with mums who worked long hours. Their dads had left the scene long ago. Rachel didn't have to watch TV documentaries to know all this.

Zodiacs wore black, of course, mostly opting for tops that had hoods. It was so boring, always rebelling by using the clichéd channels. "These kids have no imagination," she thought. "Maybe if they started cutting people's fingers off, that would be rebellion," deliberated Rachel darkly.

Interestingly, it dawned on her that the Zodiacs didn't frighten her anymore. She had met a greater evil. They didn't even come close.

One of the Zodiacs had unscrewed a light from its fitting and was about to throw it out of the window. The others were laughing raucously.

Rachel closed her eyes. They were approaching a village called Barnacle.

She was halfway there.

RACHEL SAT FUMING on the stationary train.

It was five twenty-five, and the train had stopped at a tiny station somewhere along the coast. There was the sea on one side and open countryside on the other side. The driver had locked the doors, and they were not going anywhere.

An announcement had come loud and clear over the intercom system: "This is the driver of the train. We apologise to customers for the delay, but a smoke alarm has been triggered on this train. As you may be aware, smoking is prohibited on all Griffton and South train services, and the trains are equipped with sensors that cause the train to halt if they are activated. The British Transport Police have been alerted and will arrive soon, and then we will be on our way again. In the meantime, we appreciate your patience. Again, we apologise for the delay in your service."

"Those stupid Zodiac kids," thought Rachel. "They have really done it this time. Fancy smoking in the toilets! Everyone knows the smoke detectors in the toilets are linked to the driver's cabin. He has instructions to stop the train if anyone is stupid enough to light up."

"First of all, it's written on the doors of the toilets. Second of all, you don't smoke on public transport. Third of all, these boys are so stupid. They have no brains whatsoever," fumed Rachel. Now, she was going to miss her appointment. There was no way she could miss her appointment. It just wasn't an option. Rachel was beside herself. She could feel the tears wanting to force their way out of her eyes.

"I hate them. This is so unfair," she ranted.

She sat with her arms folded for a while, then got up and tried to force the doors open. Perhaps if she could sneak out, she could run for the main road and flag down a ride.

The doors wouldn't budge.

Rachel grabbed her bag and went looking for a conductor. She would demand to leave the train. After all, they couldn't keep her on the train against her will, could they?

Ten minutes later, she had paced the length of the train and found no conductors but plenty of irate passengers. She even saw the gang of stupid Zodiac boys and gave them as evil a glare as she could muster. They were more subdued now, trapped rats, probably saving their energy for the police. The other thing about Zodiacs was they seemed to have little fear of authority and were quite happy to spend time in a police cell.

The driver's cabin was locked, and there seemed no way to contact him. She even tried banging on his door, but this only hurt her hands.

Then, the police car arrived by the side of the train, sirens blaring. It was a little over the top, thought Rachel to herself.

The time was five forty. She had to be at Lupus Street Chemist in twenty minutes.

WITH A SUPREME EFFORT on the driver's part and half a dozen extremely painful station stops, the train pulled in at Sandy Bottom Cove just twenty-five minutes late. It was five minutes to six.

Rachel leapt from the train and bolted for the exit.

Questions were rushing through her mind. Did Lupus Street Chemist close at six o'clock? How far away was it? Why hadn't she looked it up on the web? Why six o'clock, and what happens if she is a bit late? No doubt she'd find the answer to that one quickly enough. What was waiting for her at the chemist? Would anyone be there? What was this package she had to pick up, anyway?

Sandy Bottom Cove looked like any of the other sleepy villages along the coast. No one else disembarked at this stop. The station itself was empty. Rachel paused at the ticket office to ask the woman how far the chemist was. She almost cried when she heard it was just, "Left, down the road until you get to the post office, and Lupus Street is the one opposite."

Running again, Rachel went out of the station and turned left. The streets were empty by now. The few shops she could see looked like they were closed for the day. She guessed that not much happened here at Sandy Bottom Cove.

She found the post office easily. Within seconds, she was across the road and racing down Lupus Street. It was a nondescript road lined with trees.

The chemist on Lupus Street had a closed sign on the door. It was dark inside. Rachel looked at her watch. It was five minutes past six. Her heart sank.

"Well, I'm here now," thought Rachel.

She peered into the shop, seeing several aisles of the sorts of things you'd find in a chemist. She could make out rows of products: lotions and pills, combs and hairgrips. There was a counter at the back of the shop. It didn't look as though anyone was around. She was shaking slightly from fatigue and the exertion of running from the train.

She tried the door and found that it was not locked at all. Rachel took a deep breath. She prepared to step inside.

Just then, she had the feeling she was being watched.

She spun around and looked hard all around her. She glanced quickly and carefully at the windows opposite. She darted her eyes at the nearby trees, up and down the street, and even upwards at the chemist building. It was two storeys high. She saw nothing and no one. She was alone.

All she had to go on was that strange phone call she had received in the café the morning after that mysterious night. That was when she had followed her first instruction to go up to Griffton Cliff. She had then ended up on the beach.

Rachel had done what they asked, yet again, and come out on their wild goose chase. Now, she was wasting time.

She shook off her fear and ventured into the building.

She made sure she had a really good look up and down the aisles, into the corners, and over behind the counter. No one was hiding in Lupus Street Chemist, as far as she could see. She could clearly see something on the counter. It looked like a green sports bag with a gold insignia on it.

"Piece of cake," she thought.

Urging herself onwards, she walked quietly over to the counter. As she reached for the bag, she saw the legs of a man lying still at the side of the counter. She could only see his shoes and trousers from where she was standing. Rachel gasped and felt a scream rising in her throat.

CHAPTER 14

"Don't scream," reasoned a man's voice. It was gentle and soothing.

Rachel watched the legs disappear out of sight as the body was dragged along the ground into a back room. Rachel waited with no idea what to do. Maybe that guy had fainted. There was no blood. Or at least she couldn't see any. So, he couldn't be dead, she told herself. Maybe he was sleeping. Rachel told herself not to be so stupid. Everything in her wanted to scream despite being told not to. But the voice that had spoken was so calm. The calmness was infectious. Rachel found herself relaxing slightly.

"Who is he?" she heard herself asking. She waited for the answer.

"Oh, he'll be fine. Don't worry about him," the man was confident and reassuring. Rachel really wanted to believe him.

The man, Daniel Harcourt, stepped out from the back room. He was perfectly at ease with himself. He smiled at Rachel and put his hands in his pockets as if to say, I pose no threat. He was well- dressed, a handsome man in his late forties, with thinning hair. Confident and calm, Rachel thought.

She noticed him looking a little too long at her hand, where the finger had been taken. "You're the one who…" she stammered.

"What you need to do now is take the bag and go home. Don't open it, otherwise they will know. And don't even think about doing anything stupid." The man sounded bored, as though he was a tour guide, giving the same spiel for the hundredth time. "I don't want to," declared Rachel.

"Oh, don't be so stupid. Take the bag. You have no idea, have you? If I were you, I'd just do what you're told and don't ask questions."

"And if I don't?"

"Oh, Rachel, you're so naive. They have your friend, the reporter," explained Daniel slowly.

"He's not a reporter," jabbered Rachel. "He's a researcher." Then she whined, "Where is he? Please don't hurt him."

"I don't personally have him," Daniel shot back. "But would you like a bit of friendly advice? Do what you're told, and don't ask questions. Then you might stand a chance of surviving this."

"This is about Mr Samyaza, isn't it?"

"You really don't know what you're involved in, do you?" Rachel shook her head.

"Then, believe me when I tell you, he will do whatever he has to in order to get his way."

"And how about you?" asked Rachel.

"Me?" Daniel laughed. "If it's any consolation, I'm sorry about your finger and your 'researcher' friend. And I'm sorry you got involved in all this. But that's the way it is. We're all slaves to him. No one's free. You'd better start getting used to it."

Then he grew serious and thundered: "Now get out of here. Run. And wait for your orders."

Rachel grabbed the bag, which was heavier than she expected, and made her escape.

THE TOWN'S public address system amused Caleb Noble. The grey, loud hailers on tall poles were no longer in use. They had not been in use since communist times, but they still gave a strong impression of how things used to be done.

He was back in the mountains again. This time, it was the High Tatra range of mountains in northern Slovakia. Across the snowy mountains were Poland and the Czech Republic around the corner. Caleb had flown to Bratislava, the Slovakian capital, and then taken various well-worn trains north to the mountains. On the journey, he passed wooden Orthodox churches from the 16th century and vast agricultural fields.

He had been hiking through the smaller villages in the foothills, where a massive forest stretched for miles along the base of the mountains. Then, he ascended to the higher villages, Stary Smokovec, Tatranska Lomnica, and Strbske Pleso, the highest settlement in the High Tatras. He was enjoying the cold, clean air and beautiful flowers.

Like the Nepalese and the Balinese, the Slovaks loved their flowers, thought Caleb, and they always put together the most incredible flower arrangements.

A quirky little funicular, a self-contained cliff railway, took him between the towns and villages, climbing the steep inclines with ease.

It went between Hrebienok and Stary Smokovec, and the conductor punched his cardboard ticket and nodded pleasantly at him. The views from the train sang to his heart.

He noticed on a map that there was a mountain called Satan here in the High Tatras, and the idea made him shiver.

The foothills of these mountains were so completely different from the Himalayas in that the Tatras lay under miles of forest cover, with many different types of trees, plants, and grasses. Caleb felt most at home when he was out in the open, with just him and the Dunamis for company.

"Why am I here?" he asked the Dunamis. The inward

audible voice spoke inside him, saying, 'I'll tell you soon. Go for a walk up the mountains.'

"Where?" he asked.

"This way," whispered the Dunamis.

❧ 12345 ❧

CALEB WALKED past a babbling brook with beautiful purple flowers by the side. He found a long, gnarly stick with which he prodded the ground as he walked. He sipped from the cool waters, then walked on across a set of rocks. He discarded the stick and climbed a vertical ladder, which was attached to stone. This led him to an even better view of the land.

Climbing up a path that took him even higher, he was soon on a rocky ledge that brought him to the top of a steep incline. He trekked even further, climbing higher up the mountain, and saw a cloud approaching in the distance. Behind him, another cloud was also approaching fast. It looked as though the clouds had engineered a pincer movement to trap him between two prongs.

Soon, he found himself in the middle of a dense fog. He had to stop and find shelter so he didn't stumble and fall. He tried to keep warm while he waited.

❧ 12345 ❧

EVENTUALLY, the fog thinned, and he was able to go on his way again across the smooth rocks surrounded by snow. He climbed past a wall of trees to a high peak and found a natural formation resembling the eye of a needle. Scrambling to the top of the ring of rock encased in ice, he earned a breathtaking view across the five peaks of the Tatra Mountains.

Far down in a valley was a massive icy lake, the shape of a heart, edged on all sides by red-grey rocks and snow. Caleb paused for a long time, taking in the view. A light snow shower blew directly into his face, and he smiled and brushed away the worst of it.

Reluctantly, he climbed through the eye of the needle and descended the slope beyond.

At the bottom of the slope, he spied a Dream Fighter dressed in brown leather. The dark shape was surrounded by a sea of white snow.

Caleb recognised him as a Dream Fighter because he was dressed like a Dream Fighter and carried a long, sharp cane.

Besides, it was a dead giveaway that the warrior was in the same vicinity as Caleb. Wherever Caleb was, the enemy always tried to congregate and bring him down. It came with the territory, thought Caleb. Darkness and light define each other by their very natures, standing in 'contradistinction' to each other. As the light grows brighter, dark specks show up even more vividly.

He faced an enemy that never slept and would never give up. Caleb sighed quietly.

"Which way, Dunamis?" he asked under his breath. But the Dunamis was staying silent on this one for his own reasons.

This way, Caleb decided, going in the opposite direction to the Dream Fighter. In his favour was the fact he was going downhill in the opposite direction to his adversary, who would need to climb a dozen rocks to get level with him.

Caleb sang a quiet tune and disappeared down a slope. He reached the safety of a path that wound around a tall wall of rock and then curved round out of sight of the lumbering Dream Fighter.

It turned out to be a bold move which sent him down a thin and icy slope where the steps were hazardous, and he had to be very mindful of his footing. One wrong move could have landed his ankle in a pothole made of ice and rock and rendered him unable to walk.

AT THE BOTTOM of the long slope, he found himself in a valley of melting snow, with streams of water beginning to flow downwards to feed distant waterfalls and rivers.

He followed these for some time, seeing no one behind him, no ghostly apparitions in black. This path, he felt, wound back to Strbske Pleso, where many hikers and walkers started their adventures. After a few more hours of walking, everything would be green again. Lining the paths, he would see the thick yellow vertical strands of dry grass and the dry and broken trunks of trees.

CALEB STOPPED by an outcropping of green growth by a rippling pool of water, where he rested his tired feet. A map of brown tree roots etched the ground. He looked at his reflection in the water, seeing the familiar square jaw and closely cropped grey hair. When he stood up to leave, he came face to face with the Dream Fighter.

The man had a fierce countenance and looked in no mood to make friends. Still, Caleb would try.

"Ah, my friend," smiled Caleb. "What brings you here?"

"The same to you, enemy of Samyaza," grunted the warrior. "You come with me."

Caleb shrugged and sought direction from the Dunamis. No advice was forthcoming. Caleb frowned, knowing trouble was ahead. A fist landed in his stomach.

"Come now," barked the fighting man.

THEY PUT Caleb into a small cell with a view of the forest through wooden bars. He sought the voice of the Dunamis ceaselessly but heard nothing.

Nothing would happen without the creator allowing it. He

knew this for certain. But that didn't mean he was exempt from pain in this world. Far from it – the path he had chosen was beset with trouble and persecution. His bleeding face right now was proof he would endure hardship and trouble as he travelled.

The Dream Fighters had beaten him, mainly to put some sort of fear into him, but they discovered that this was fruitless. Caleb vexed them with his patience, and the man seemed to fear nothing.

He was confident he had the Dunamis to guide and protect him, equip and empower him. Because of this, he had learned the secret of being completely at peace. He knew as a fact that he was indestructible while the creator still had work for him to do.

At the moment, his job was to find out the whereabouts of Rachel Race, the girl who was the key to what was happening in Makalu, Nepal. When his job was done, well, that was a different matter. But he didn't feel as though his time was up yet. Not at all.

He sat cross-legged on the floor of his cell, patiently watching the forest while his captors grew increasingly agitated. He heard them arguing amongst themselves.

It was the usual thing. They were vying for a position so they would be seen by Samyaza as having served him the best. That was why they had captured and beaten Caleb. They were all trying to be the top dog. But they were wasting their time. Samyaza only wanted one thing: the destruction of their souls.

In reality, he couldn't care less about their petty rivalries.

After a couple of hours in the cell, the Dunamis finally spoke to Caleb, bathing him with the healing balm of his presence and telling him to ask for Jorge. Caleb knew he needed to act now.

"I'd like to see Jorge," called Caleb. "Please bring Jorge to me right now," he added for clarity.

"You shut up. We bring you no one and nothing," spat the man who was posted outside his cell.

The guard sat heavily on a wooden stool. He was a nasty-looking warrior all in black, with a spiky insignia on his chest that no doubt told the others how violent and disagreeable he could be.

Caleb tried to change his line. "If you bring Jorge to me, I could tell you why I'm here."

The guard ignored him and started to fish a paper out of a leather pouch and fill it with tobacco.

"How about you let Jorge decide for himself?" Caleb tried. The man started to shift uneasily in his chair. "If you don't get Jorge, and I really need to talk to him, well, that would be bad for you," reasoned Caleb.

"How do you know Jorge anyway?" asked the Dream Fighter in a gruff voice, pronouncing Jorge in two long syllables: "hor-hay" and rolling the 'r' in the middle of the name.

Caleb smiled peacefully at him. "I'd be grateful if you could get Jorge. I'd like to speak to him, my brother."

The Dream Fighter spat on the ground and growled. "You're no brother of mine," he cursed, but he got up and stomped off just the same. "We bring you no one and nothing," he roared again over his shoulder.

Caleb had absolutely no idea who Jorge was, but he trusted the Dunamis. All the while, Caleb was begging the Dunamis to give him more information. "Tell me something, anything," he begged.

At length, the guard came back with another Dream Fighter. This one was dressed in red leather with black patches. He had long black hair tied at the back of his skull and small, dark eyes set far apart.

"Okay, we will bring you, Jorge," informed this Dream Fighter, who was apparently the one in charge.

"Very good," retorted Caleb.

Then he looked away at the forest through the bars of the cell. "Dunamis," he said silently, "you really have to give me something else to go on, or I'm in real trouble."

CHAPTER 15

Back home, Rachel had a sore arm from carrying the heavy green sports bag. She also had a fierce desire to know what was inside it.

Her suspicion was they were using her as a mule to carry a large quantity of drugs from one place to another. The fact she had to go to a pharmacist to get the package was a bit of a give-away, she thought.

"Are they really holding Lake Emerson captive? Why would they kidnap him anyway? Shall I tell the police? What should I tell them?" she asked herself.

She got home late in the evening and faced a potentially awkward conversation with her dad. He was eating a pizza in front of the television and, thankfully, didn't ask about the bag. He looked tired and barely glanced at her when she came in. As ever, he had a drink in his hand.

"Save a piece for me. I'll be back down in a minute," called Rachel as she nonchalantly took the green bag upstairs to her bedroom. The best thing for her to do was to act normal, she decided.

She came down and sat on the double sofa. Her dad was sitting in his comfortable chair and continued to watch the box.

She grabbed a slice of Hawaiian pizza, realising that she was ravenous.

"My favourite, how thoughtful," exclaimed Rachel.

Her dad turned and smiled at her. "Sorry, love, how have you been?" he asked tenderly.

It was like he'd thrown Rachel a curve ball. She didn't really know how to answer his question. She could choose to tell him about the lights on Griffton Cliff and how she had experienced her mother's presence and then spent a night on Griffton beach. The freshest adventure was her journey to the chemist in Sandy Bottom. Being assaulted by the scary tramp was also high on the list of things she could tell her dad.

Then, there was the way she had been recruited into the ranks of the forces of darkness and evil.

"Not too bad, dad. You?" enquired Rachel. "Yeah. Not too bad," he replied.

"So, what are we watching?" asked Rachel.

"Oh, nothing really. These two girls here are really into their fitness, bodybuilding, and all that. This one here in the pink, she's only twenty-one, can you believe it? To be honest, I was just about to switch it off," mumbled her dad.

"Yeah, right," Rachel grinned.

"I got a film out," her dad professed hopefully. "What's that then?"

"Apparently, it's meant to be really good. It's about this guy who gets recruited to do secret missions for the CIA, but one of his missions goes wrong, and they can't tell anyone they sent him out. Otherwise, they're in trouble. Want to see it?"

Rachel raised her eyebrows. "Okay, I'll give it a go," she said.

HALFWAY THROUGH THE FILM, Rachel noticed her dad was asleep. It was then that she spied the corner of an envelope under the rug near the door. She wondered how long it had been there and who it was for. Curiously, she crept over and turned it over in her hands. She saw it was addressed to her. She rarely got mail, so this was intriguing. She dearly hoped it wasn't from them: the bad guys.

Rachel took it upstairs, leaving her father asleep in front of the film.

She sat on her bed and tore the top off the envelope. She discovered lots of printed sheets inside. On the top page was a large yellow sticky note with some scribbled words. It was from Lake. She relaxed.

"Hi Rach, this is Lake. Sorry, I haven't called. I've been busy following up on some of that crazy madness we talked about in the library. Looks like there's more to it than meets the eye! Fascinating stuff. Let's talk soon."

She flipped through the pages and felt a cold dread descend on her.

AT THE TOP of the pile was some information on this Samyaza character. Apparently, he was one of the Grigori, a group of fallen angels mentioned in the Bible and other writings called the Apocrypha. The Grigori were also known as "Watchers" – *egregoroi* in ancient Greek.

There were two hundred of these angels, with names like Azazyel, Akibeel, Tamiel, and Ramuel. They were pretty names, Rachel felt. But these characters weren't so pretty themselves when it came down to it. Samyaza was their leader, and they slept with human women, who gave birth to a race of savage giants known as the Nephilim.

There was a quote from the book of Genesis: "When men began to multiply on earth and daughters were born to them, the sons of heaven saw how beautiful the daughters of man were, and so they took for their wives as many of them as they chose. Then the Lord said: "My spirit shall not remain in man forever, since he is but flesh. His days shall comprise one hundred and twenty years." There were Nephilim on the earth in those days, and also after that, when the sons of God slept with the daughters of men, who bore them sons. These became mighty men of old, men of renown."

Rachel read on, trying to work out why exactly Lake had sent her all this strange stuff.

She found some more information on Samyaza. Here it was again: these Watchers, angels apparently dispatched to Earth to watch over the humans, begin to lust after human women. Prodded on by their leader Samyaza, they defected en masse to marry and live among the humans.

Their kids, the Nephilim, pillaged the earth and endangered humanity, and Samyaza, Azazel, and the others became corrupt and taught their human hosts to make weapons out of metal so they could kill each other. Then God sent the Great Flood to rid the earth of the Nephilim and all the evil, corruption, and violence he saw in the world. But he sent the angel Uriel ahead to warn Noah so the human race wouldn't be totally wiped out by the move, and a remnant would remain. The hope of something better.

Rachel remembered the story about Noah and the ark and how he gathered up all the animals and escaped the rains by living in a big boat. It must have been really noisy, she imagined. It was probably really smelly, too.

Lake's research went on to say that after the flood, the Grigori- Watchers were bound up "in the valleys of the Earth" until Judgement Day.

SHE REALLY STARTED to pay attention when Lake's notes started to talk about the mountains. There were some myths about Samyaza that hadn't been formally recorded but were passed down as part of an oral tradition in Nepal and also parts of South America, including Bolivia.

They said Samyaza and his gang were bound in the valleys adjacent to the mountains, possibly the Andes or the Himalayas.

Rachel sat bolt upright as she turned the page and saw a printout of the mountain in her dreams.

There was the familiar double peak and sheets of white ice and snow. It was the mountain; there was no doubt about it. The mountain had filled her with awe and dread, and now it was staring out at her from an Internet printout.

'Makalu,' said the caption, 'is a member of the Himalayan Mountain range, which is home to all fourteen of the world's highest peaks.'

"No kidding," gasped Rachel. She checked the time and saw it was before ten o'clock at night.

The man at the chemist had said, "We have your friend, 'the reporter.'"

She had to call Lake to find out if it was true.

She got the handset and called Lake's mobile number. There was no answer. She began to grow anxious. She tried his home number, and his mum answered.

It was the first time Rachel had spoken to her, and she tried to hide her nervousness by being super-polite.

"Hello Mrs Emerson? This is Rachel, a friend of Lake's," she jabbered.

"Hello, Rachel. Do call me Anne. Yes, Lake has mentioned you," replied Anne Emerson.

"He has?" said Rachel, feeling wrong-footed. "Sorry to call so late," she added, remembering her manners.

"That's fine: we're all up. Except Lake, that is. He's still out, I'm afraid. He texted to say he's gone out to the pub," Anne informed her.

"Oh, okay," muttered Rachel, crestfallen. She said goodbye.

Half of her was glad he was okay and not kidnapped, as that man had said. But half of her was annoyed he wasn't answering his phone. Plus, he had gone down the pub, but he hadn't been there last night when she wanted him to be.

"Boys," she lamented under her breath.

SHE TURNED BACK to her pile of papers. There was still more to get through. Another strand of folklore coming out of the Himalayas was about some sort of doorway between worlds. It was some sort of portal. The myth was that this portal in the mountains led between this world and the spirit world.

Under the right circumstances, it would be possible to open the portal, and at that point, the Grigori and their Nephilim would be able to break their supernatural chains and return to the earth to wreak havoc and reorder the world through tyranny. That was according to the myth.

So, this Samyaza was trying to escape from the place where he was bound, and to do this, he had to somehow open the portal and bring about the end of the world.

It sounded like 'crazy madness' to Rachel, as Lake had said.

Then, it dawned on her that Lake was making fun of her. He had spun a yarn as a practical joke. What was worse, she had been momentarily taken in by all this stuff.

She was disappointed Lake would think of playing such a nasty trick on her. He was such a storyteller, and he obviously had a juvenile sense of humour. It should have been enough to say he didn't believe her about all the strange stuff that had happened and leave it at that. But to go so many steps further and make up all of this fantasy was just beyond the pale. Then fancy disappearing down the pub like that. He was such a coward.

Suddenly, Rachel realised she really didn't know that much about Lake Emerson. He was a nice guy, more than nice. She did like him very much, but if he was going to make fun of her like this, then how could she bear to spend any time with him?

To think she had trusted him with some of her rawest emotions. It was too much to bear.

Rachel stuffed the pages back into the envelope and threw it on the floor.

Then she saw the green sports bag by the wardrobe. It was bulky, heavy, and foreboding. Was there any truth to any of this stuff?

The bag suggested there was.

She closed her eyes. She really needed some sleep, and she had work tomorrow. She curled up on the bed, but nothing she tried would shut down her brain.

THE DREAM FIGHTERS took their time bringing Jorge to Caleb. When he finally arrived, Jorge looked like a wholly unremarkable man with a thin face and a long, droopy moustache. Dressed in the Dream Fighters' uniform of a leather tunic and body protector, Jorge stood just a little over five feet tall, shorter than the others, and his muscles were knotty and small.

Caleb regarded him for a while, waiting on the Dunamis. Finally, information came to him like a flood, and Caleb opened his mouth and delivered the message.

"Jorge, you serve Samyaza and have done since you were a boy. You serve him, but you hate him. You live in a small hut that is one hour's walk south of here. You are not from here. You are from Portugal originally. Your son is sick."

Caleb paused but soon continued, "Your son is Emmanuel. He is sick. Did you know that Emmanuel, as well as being King Emmanuel of Portugal, also means 'God with us'? Your son has a fever, but when you return to him, by the power of the Dunamis, Emmanuel will be restored to health."

"Impossible," stammered Jorge, tears rolling down his cheeks. "You won't find your Samyaza doing such an act. Now, tell me where Rachel Race can be found. And tell me now," smiled Caleb.

"The girl is in a coastal town in England. Its name is Griffton. Is my son really healed?" asked Jorge in a thin voice. His eyes were wet.

"I would not lie to you," stated Caleb.

He turned to the wooden bars of the cell and closed his eyes. As he opened them, he watched the bats explode outwards, sending tiny wooden splinters into the forest. The Dream Fighters stood rooted to the spot, watching closely. The large guard felt his cigarette burn down to his fingers as he stared but was unable to move.

"Now I will go," chirped Caleb, and leapt out of the window. They had no intention of stopping him.

CHAPTER 16

By the time morning came, Rachel had got out of bed and walked over to the sports bag no less than five times.

The streetlight through the open window made the bag shine with an eerie glow. On her final wander over to the bag, Rachel could resist it no longer. She carefully unzipped it and looked inside as though she half expected it to explode in her face.

Just as she feared, the bag contained a huge polythene packet filled with grey powder. She felt her shoulders sag. Nestled beside the polythene bag was a white envelope. It had her name on it.

She snatched it up, consumed with a burning desire to know what it said and why it was in there. Suspecting she was about to be drawn into yet another of their games, she stared at the paper rectangle for several moments.

At last, she could take it no more and decided to rip it open. "Didn't you know that curiosity killed the cat?" the note began.

It was double-spaced and typed in a nondescript typeface. Of course, it had the little picture of the four-fingered hand. Rachel pulled a face.

"Your third assignment is to deliver this bag to Lower Ledge

Crossing on Griffton Cliff at six o'clock. Don't tell a soul," the note declared.

"Great," moaned Rachel to the bag. "Just deliver the bag. Who's going to die this time?" She hoped to goodness it wasn't going to be Lake.

☙ 12345 ❧

WORK TOOK her mind off things to some extent. She found herself unable to talk freely with Iona because of the threats this Samyaza character was making. All the cloak and dagger "don't tell a soul" stuff was paying off, she thought. She really didn't fancy losing another finger or her hand. She also didn't want to endanger Lake's life any more than she had already by telling him about Samyaza.

So, for the time being, she had to play ball and do what they said. Iona wasn't generally into having any deep conversations, which was fine with her. In fact, it was one of the reasons why Rachel liked her so much, along with her taste in music and her shamelessly hippy dress sense.

It had been such a long week already, with the scary man grabbing her on Saturday, Griffton Cliff on Sunday, Lupus Street Chemist on Monday, and tonight's assignment crawling ever closer. Were they going to find something for her to do every day? If that was the case, Rachel didn't know how much of it she could take before she just collapsed with exhaustion.

What she wanted most of all was some decent sleep. What would be ideal is a hotel bed with a thick feather duvet where no one could find her, and she could sleep for a month.

☙ 12345 ❧

LARA CALLED RACHEL AT LUNCHTIME, catching her on the shop landline just as she was about to wander outside to watch the sea.

"Have you seen Lake?"

"What do you mean?" asked Rachel.

"Well, Joel hasn't seen him. He's tried calling but can't get hold of him. He was meant to come to the Pirate's Paradise on Sunday. Since then, no one knows where he is. It's like, a mystery."

"Well, I haven't seen him since Saturday."

"Saturday? You never mentioned Saturday," objected Lara.

"I don't have to tell you everything," snapped Rachel. "Anyway, you've been busy packing and stuff."

"But I'm your best friend! Was it, like, a date or something?"

"No. Do you remember that guy in the shop I told you about who followed me to the library?"

"Not really," said Lara.

"The tramp, who stalked me? I told you about him."

"Oh yeah, him! I remember."

"Well, Lake was in the library as well, and he sort of rescued me," Rachel mumbled.

"You definitely left out that part when you told me on Sunday," teased Lara.

"Well, there you go."

"So, was it, like, a date then? Did you kiss him?" asked Lara. "I told you," Rachel shot back.

"No, you didn't," Lara objected.

"I'd just had, like, a really big scare with this awful man and…" Rachel checked herself to make sure she didn't reveal anything about Samyaza or his assignments or anything else that might lose her a hand or a best friend. "Like I said, he sort of rescued me."

"Well, tell me this: did he say – on your 'not-a-date' – he was going anywhere?" asked Lara, sounding exasperated.

"No, he didn't. And I haven't seen him since or talked to him."

"That bad?" asked Lara.

"Stop digging. It wasn't a date, Lemur," insisted Rachel.

"Well, you know, Racoon, it's kind of strange no one can get hold of him, that's all I'm saying. So when he calls you to ask you out for another 'not-a-date,' make sure to tell me. Then I can tell Joel, and Joel can kick Lake's rollerblading butt. See ya!"

"See ya, Lemur," said Rachel.

"They've got Lake," she said to herself. "I have to do something."

RACHEL SPENT the rest of her lunch break doing detective work to find out where Lake was. Lake's work, the Griffton News, seemed to think he was taking some holiday. This was according to the editorial assistant, Kimberley.

His mum, Anne Emerson, had received a text from Lake saying he had gone away on assignment. He had gone for a few days to Polcombe, which was the next large town along the coast. He also said the paper was putting him up in a nice hotel. Although this was unusual, Anne was proud of her son and reckoned he was in line for a promotion soon.

"And this text came from his mobile phone?" quizzed Rachel. "Yes, that's right," said Mrs Emerson.

"I haven't been able to get through to his mobile," muttered Rachel, mainly to herself.

"I expect he's busy with his research," said Mrs Emerson proudly.

Rachel wasn't convinced. She decided not to mention the paper had told her he was on holiday. Coupled with the fact the man in Lupus Street Chemist had said 'they' were holding Lake, the situation looked bleak.

She wracked her brain for a plan but failed miserably to do anything other than feel anxious and unhappy.

AGAINST HER BETTER NATURE, Rachel found herself on the green bus to Lower Ledge Crossing on Griffton Cliff. She was sitting at the back of the bus again, with the heavy sports bag between her feet on the floor, sweating lightly. There was a different driver from last time, and this time around, the bus was packed full of commuters.

She stared at them, trying to find something out of the ordinary that might give them away as belonging to the enemy. The enemy were the people who were manipulating her like she was a dog to send fetching and carrying.

There were a couple of lonely shop workers: girls like her. They were going home after their shifts, where they probably spent the whole day on their feet, serving customers who were short on time and manners. She saw lots of businesspeople, men, and women, in smart suits and skirts. Some of these lived in the big houses on the outskirts. There were a couple of pensioners out for the day.

The bus emptied slowly as it approached the cliff, and fifteen minutes before it got to Lower Ledge Crossing, she was the only person on the bus again. She was alone except for the driver and the mystery parcel in the green sports bag.

Rachel did not think she had ever felt this isolated from her friends and family. There was no one she could talk to or confide in. Even Lake, her new friend, had been taken. He was the one whom she wanted to trust the most in all of this. Lara was going, going, gone; her dad was never going to be there for her – not really. As for everyone else, well, there wasn't an 'everyone else' to speak of. How did she ever get to be this alone? The pain of it made her bones feel heavy.

Then she arrived at the final stop, where the bus would turn around and leave her behind, heading for the safety and warmth of the city.

With a strong sense of déjà vu, Rachel stood and watched the bus drive out of sight down the hill. Fortunately, it was still light, but she was alone and vulnerable. Plus, she had no idea where she was meant to go.

It was five minutes to six, which meant she'd made it to the appointed place comfortably early. This should mean she could afford to be relaxed, but the sense of foreboding made this difficult.

She looked around, seeing nothing and no one of note. There was the aroma of smoke in the air, perhaps from a bonfire or chimney stack. There were very few houses on the cliff, but it surely must be coming from one of them, she thought.

At exactly six o'clock, a red and black car pulled up near her. Her heart beat faster. Two men were in the car, a tanned man with a lined face and a younger man with dyed peroxide blond hair. The older man stayed behind the wheel.

The younger man exited the car, leaving the door open. "Are you going to kidnap me as well?" Rachel thought but said nothing.

She gaped as she watched the man, who was wearing a dark shirt and jeans, come up to her. He grinned and leaned towards her. Rachel closed her eyes. When she opened them again, she saw the man walking towards the car with the green sports bag. He had taken it from her. She had actually forgotten about the thing in her dread. No words had been exchanged.

The car drove off down the hill, and Rachel heard herself calling out: "What have you done with Lake? What am I meant to do now?" She rubbed her maimed left hand as she shouted, but the men had already gone, leaving a plume of dust in the air.

As the words left her, that calm boldness grabbed hold of her and urged her to run after the car. It was her only connection with Samyaza and his secret army of hoods. She yielded to her impulse and felt a spark of adrenalin jolt her into life. Wasting no time at all, she raced off in pursuit.

She sprinted down the hill and felt the hard road surface beneath her cushioned trainers. Using the balls of her feet to launch herself forward, Rachel ran as fast as she could.

After a few minutes of running, she caught sight of the red and black car further along the road, down below her. It was turning into a lane that led towards the woods that nestled against the base of the cliff.

"Got you," she panted quietly and grinned.

But very quickly, she realised there was very little she could do to 'get' anybody when it came down to it. Particularly two large and dangerous-looking men in a fast car.

RACHEL FOLLOWED THE ROAD DOWNHILL, past a set of rails that existed to stop cars from flying off the edge of the steep road. She walked past tall, rugged trees and a small log cabin. She saw the sun start to descend in the west, ahead and left of her. The road eventually brought her to the mouth of the lane, which led into the woods at the base of the cliff, where the red and black car had sneaked away.

She stopped at the entrance, seeing it was a private road with a loose gravel path with branches poking out along the way.

"What are you doing, Rachel?" she asked herself, desperately trying to convince herself to go back onto the main road and wait for a bus.

She had the option of cutting her losses and calling the police now that she had seen three of the men who were involved in these strange activities. Four men, if you included the tramp who had stalked her to the library. She could describe all of them if it came to a police lineup or assembling a photofit picture. She knew their faces, what they wore, what colour their hair was. Now she knew where they lived.

Then the phrase came back to her: "Don't tell a soul." She was alone in this, and the police were not equipped to help her. They would never believe her if she told them about the black panther that had attacked her in the hospital. How could she explain the white dancing lights on the cliff? Or the visions of the mountains in Nepal or the strong man with short hair and black sunglasses. They would lock her up or think she was on drugs.

Anyway, how can you catch an enemy that is more spirit than flesh using physical means? It's impossible. This Samyaza was hard to pin down because he had many faces and yet no face. He could cause things to happen: panthers to fly through windows. Then, like the wind, he would move on.

No, she was on her own now because no one would believe her. It was down to her to find out the answers to all of her questions: why they had taken her finger, why they had involved her in all of these assignments, and why they had chosen her at all.

Tentatively, she crept down the lane into the dark forest, which crowded the path ahead on both sides.

There were no streetlights here or even dancing lights. But the fading sunlight helped her to stay on the path. As she went deeper in, the trees grew thicker and taller, and spiky bushes lined the path. The stench of smoke was also growing stronger in her nostrils as Rachel moved on. She started talking to herself to encourage herself and fight back the fear.

Every so often, she heard rustling on one side or the other or above her. It made her freeze for a few seconds to see if she could spot the lion or the bear that was about to eat her.

Progress was slow as Rachel inched down the private road. But in time, it opened up to reveal a large manor house at the end of the lane. It was a dark old mansion with several wings and a complicated roof system that held it all together. A wide garden lay before the dark building, and an unkempt hedge hemmed in the grounds.

"So, this is your hideout," she murmured. Fear wanted her to run. Curiosity drove her forward.

"Curiosity killed the cat," the note had said. It might have been some sort of warning and possibly a reference to Lake and what he had discovered about Samyaza. But deep down, Rachel wanted and needed to know the answers. She couldn't stop now until she knew everything, and besides, she was much too far along the road to turn back.

Rachel held her breath and scanned the house from one end to the other. She spotted a ground-floor window on one side. It was open slightly. She decided it was the best place to eavesdrop.

Then she steadied her nerves and crept towards it, trying to stay close to the bushes.

CHAPTER 17

Rachel made it to the side of the house without being seen. It had been a long trip along the hedge. But she had benefited from the failing light and the fact the men inside were not expecting her.

With her heart thumping in her chest, she pressed against the wall and got as close up to the window as she dared. She strained to listen for any noises over the pounding of her heart.

A moaning sound was discernible from inside the house. The sounds were eerie and irregular at first. But then they fell into a pattern. It sounded to her like chanting. Men were chanting in some funny language. Rachel stood still and tried to make out the words.

"*Sor-cah-yah. Hom-kii-ta-ray. Who-par-key. Yor-way-mah. Sam-yaz-eh.*"

She recognised that last word. Had it been some form of 'Samyaza'? She was pretty certain it was.

Rachel felt herself stiffen.

"*Son-kii-mah. Sor-cah-yah. Bah-loo-fey,*" continued the chanting.

THE HOODED FIGURES had shoved Lake into some sort of storage room. There were piles of heavy wooden boxes at the edges and in the corners of the high-ceilinged room. Apart from a small, barred window and the door through which he had entered, there was no escape. It was a good thing they had not bound him. But it was clear he wasn't going anywhere.

He was also getting hungry. He had not eaten much since breakfast yesterday. He regretted he had not eaten that peanut butter sandwich. The one he'd left on a plate on his front room floor.

Lake spent a lot of yesterday in a daze, trying desperately to remember how he got from his house to this place. He remembered walking up his stairs into the cloud of mist, which had lights on it. But he must have passed out shortly afterwards.

The rest of yesterday was pretty hazy. He felt as though he had slept for a long time on the floor of the storeroom.

Today, he spent most of his time shouting for attention. He smashed up all the empty boxes he could find and tried to get the bars off the window. He couldn't actually open the full boxes with his bare hands because he needed a crowbar for that. There were some heavy crates which he could just about move along the ground. Anyway, his actions had achieved little.

At lunchtime, the hooded men had fed him an insubstantial meal of bread and fruit, busying themselves in another part of the house.

He worked out there were two or three of them, but one or two others had visited them a couple of times during the day. He managed to keep his fear at bay by writing the news story of his abduction in his head and concocting various feature spinoffs. The journalist in him was breaking out, and the thought thrilled him. He had all these dreams of being a writer. If he ever got to live through this, he could pen a book, he joked to himself.

Towards the end of the day, he was hanging onto the bars of the window, trying to see if anyone was out there. He figured he was in a house in the woods. But he had no clue how far from home he was. Or if he was even in Griffton.

The men in the house didn't seem to care what he did as long as he didn't cause them any trouble. They also didn't care to answer any of his questions. Looking on the bright side, they had not harmed him yet, apart from locking him in this room and feeding him prison food.

This time, when he hung onto the bars and hauled himself up to look out, he nearly cried. His own cute-as-a-button Rachel Race was creeping along the hedge towards the house. He could barely believe it.

He could see her approaching the window along the wall, stepping carefully and staying in the shadows. She looked small against the tall bushes, but the fact she was here filled him with great hope.

As soon as he saw her, he wanted to call out to her and tell her he was there. But he knew if he did that, the men might bolt out of the house and grab her, too. No, he couldn't do that.

As he delayed, his arms grew heavier. They were tiring from the exertion of holding his body up to the bars. No matter how hard he tried to whisper, Rachel didn't turn his way.

"Does she even know I'm here? What's she doing at the house anyway?" he wondered.

Lake had a Eureka moment and quickly let himself down. He pulled a purple and orange nightclub flyer out of his back pocket. The men hadn't taken it when they searched him because it had fit so snugly in his pocket against the curve of his bottom.

He quickly made a paper aeroplane out of the flier, put it in his mouth, and hauled himself up again. Pressing himself against the wall, he grabbed the plane and floated it between the bars and out of the window. He saw it sail outwards but had no idea if Rachel was even paying attention. "So much for that," he thought.

Just before his arms gave way and he slipped back down into

the storeroom, he saw two of his captors converge on Rachel from both sides. One of them grabbed her by the shoulder.

"WHAT DO YOU WANT WITH ME?" asked Rachel, desperately.

They had her sitting on a wooden chair in the middle of a large, empty room. The men didn't have much of an eye for interior design. Lining the bare walls were boxes of tools, with nuts and bolts and various bits of engineering materials strewn across the floor. The place had the odour of engine oil and wood shavings. A three-headed light fitting hung in the middle of the room, but only one light bulb worked.

The young man with the bottle-blonde hair sneered menacingly at her. "You're a pretty little thing, aren't you?" he said.

There was no one else in the room. "What's a pretty thing like you doing out here in the middle of nowhere? We could have a lot of fun, you know."

Rachel tried to stop herself from shaking and noticed for the first time a faint scar that ran down the man's cheek, from his eye to his mouth.

"You could let me go," Rachel found herself saying.

"Yeah, we could do. But why don't you stick around for a while? You might find it interesting."

Another man walked in. It was the older man who was in the car with this one, the tanned man with the lined face. The older man was wearing a strange cloak, a long black cape with a hood. "Forget about her. We have work to do," he growled, with a voice that had seen far too many cigarettes. Then he left the room.

Rachel looked up at the scar-faced man.

IN ANOTHER PART of the house, Lake had been reinvigorated by Rachel's arrival. He paced around the storeroom, hoping desperately that they weren't going to hurt Rachel.

He formed a plan in his head but had no idea whether it would work in practice. When he was a young boy at school, his gang of friends used to play a trick on the other kids. He would engage the unsuspecting victim in conversation. Meanwhile, a friend would go around behind the person and crouch down on all fours. Then Lake would shove them suddenly, with both of his palms aimed at their chest. This would send them tumbling backwards over the accomplice. Then, both of them would run off, only to play the trick on the next person. It was very childish, but it might just work, thought Lake.

The first part of the plan involved Lake tapping on the pipe with his shoe in his hand, partly to make a loud noise and partly to irritate them enough to come into the room. It struck him while he was banging away that they might come mob-handed. If they did, he was stuck. He couldn't push two people over two sets of boxes at the same time. He wasn't a ninja.

The tapping part of the plan worked, and he eventually heard somebody approaching his door. He had lined up some of the less heavy boxes to the left of the door, having pushed them across. He stood to the right of the door as it swung towards him. The beauty of his plan was its simplicity.

It was the first time Lake had seen one of their faces. This man wore the robes they all wore. When he opened the door, Lake could clearly see he was a man in his sixties with a tanned and heavily lined face.

"What's all the noise?" the man growled. That was the last thing he said because he went tumbling backwards over a stack of empty boxes and hit his head on the ground. Lake laughed, just like he always had when he was a kid in the playground.

Then he took the opportunity to run out of the door as his captor kicked his legs into the air.

MEANWHILE, the young man had decided to give Rachel a scare. He kicked her chair hard so that it slid back against the wall and then pulled on his hood. She saw that his cloak was embroidered with strange signs, like zodiac signs, but with elements of Eastern design as well. "Such beautiful symbols," she thought.

When he started chanting, his voice was very low. It had a hypnotic quality to it.

"*Sor-cah-yah. Hom-kii-ta-ray. Who-par-key. Yor-way-mah. Sam-yaz-eh*," intoned the young man.

His chanting troubled Rachel first of all, but then it sent her into a relaxed stupor. When the cloud of dust with the little lights in it finally appeared, Rachel gasped.

Of course, she had seen this before when the lights had led her up to Griffton Cliff and put on a show for her. She didn't understand what she was seeing but was again transfixed by the beauty of the dancing lights. They looked like tiny angels, spinning and dancing just for her.

She watched the dust cloud settle around the man. She half expected her mother's face to appear again and was disappointed when it didn't. Instead, she saw half a dozen alien faces appear in the mist. They had blazing eyes and ravenous jaws. Flashes of violent anger crossed their faces as they rolled their heads.

One of them, his face contorted as though in pain, jerked his head and stared at her, stock still.

Rachel screamed.

LAKE HEARD the scream as he left the room he had been held in. He recognised it as Rachel's voice. It came from a distance, across the other side of the house. Lake closed the door of the storeroom and slipped the heavy bolt into place.

Then he was off and running down a long, dark corridor that was bare except for a solitary picture on the wall.

As he ran down the hall, he felt his legs grow lighter. He looked down at the long carpet beneath him and saw it was moving further away from him. He was running, but his steps were carrying him up into the air.

Panicking now, he kicked his legs wildly but saw with horror that he was still rising upwards. It was as though a harness were lifting him into the air.

At the end of the corridor, he saw another hooded figure step out. It was a tall, thin figure with a dark grey cloak, chanting and pointing at him. A line of yellow static ascended from the man's finger and wound itself around Lake. Soon, he was utterly bound by the strange yellow lightning, curled up by the ceiling and twisting around to shake himself free.

"This is not happening," he told himself over and over again.

He eyed the tall, dark figure at the end of the corridor. "This is some sort of trick. It's some sort of magic trick – smoke and mirrors. I've seen David Blaine online. This can all be explained rationally," he said to himself.

All the while, he watched the carpet, which was some twelve feet below him, and hoped he wasn't going to tumble down to the ground.

"Rachel," he shouted as loudly as he could.

CHAPTER 18

aniel was pacing again. He was in a restaurant waiting for his veal to be cooked to perfection. It was called Soliloquy and was one of Griffton's finest establishments. The dishes were selected carefully and changed each day because all the produce was local and fresh. Daniel always made a point to order something that wasn't on the menu to keep the kitchen staff on their toes. They never missed a beat.

He had his phone pressed to his ear and was muttering, "Pick up the phone, you idiots. Pick up…" His fingers fiddled with his pink silk tie.

Finally, they answered the phone. It was a grumpy man with a deep voice. "Yeah?"

"The boss says let her go. He's far from pleased that you're keeping her there. He also wants you to know he does not, under any circumstances, want her harmed, do you hear?"

"What?" asked the man with the deep voice. He was the tanned man with the lined face.

"Are you deaf?" snapped Daniel.

"No, I just don't get it. She comes here spying on us, creeping around, and Samyaza just wants us to let her go? Why should we? Jerry wants to have some fun with her."

"Well, tell Jerry to find someone else to bother. There's been a change of plan."

"What do you mean?"

Daniel's tone hardened. "She's going to carry out Project GM for us."

"The girl? Are you serious?"

"This is Samyaza we're talking about. You know he's serious," said Daniel.

"Well, okay, if that's what he wants. We'll give her the bag for GM. It's almost ready."

"Good." Daniel checked again to see if there was anyone else loitering around in the lobby area of the restaurant. It was clear.

"There's one more thing. Samyaza says not to kill the boy yet. Keep him contained. We still need him as a lever."

"Will do," growled the man.

Daniel switched off his phone and flipped it closed.

He hoped Samyaza wasn't tuning in or paying attention. The second command about the boy had come directly from Daniel, who had made it up on the spot.

There was something about the girl, Rachel Race, that had touched his heart. He really wanted to help her, though he knew it was futile. He also knew that defying Samyaza would end badly for him. But he was almost past caring.

IT WAS a strange and frightening journey back into the valley for Rachel. They had bundled her into the back of their car and driven speedily down the cliff road and into Griffton Centre. But as they drove, the nightmare creatures from the dark cloud kept popping into her mind. It was almost as though she was living and moving inside a strange vision, reality overlaid with the supernatural. But though she feared these creatures of the night, they had not harmed her, and the men who served them appeared to be letting her go.

She watched Griffton city centre wash over them as they passed the familiar traffic light stops and roundabouts. She gazed at the neon lights and the nightlife. She breathed in the fast-food joints and the distant salty sea.

She knew the men's faces now and where their hideout was, up near Lower Ledge Crossing. The peroxide-blond man was even driving the car. How hard would it be to signal someone and get them arrested?

But they had the upper hand in everything. If this was a game of chess, then she had lost her queen and most of her back row. Don't tell a soul. They could get to her anywhere. They had Lake Emerson.

Suddenly, she sat upright in her chair. She had seen a paper aeroplane. The paper aeroplane had floated out of the window at the house, and Lake was behind it. It was made of purple and orange cards. It was the same purple and orange as the flyer they had picked up on one of their 'not-a-date' meetings. It was a night when they had met up to hang out and talk. The flyer was advertising a retro jungle night at the Kafka Klub down on the beach road. The Kafka Klub!

Lake had tried to send a signal to her, and she'd totally missed it. He was trapped.

"You have Lake Emerson back at the house. You're holding him, aren't you?" she asked, overcome with indignation.

"I don't know what you're talking about," said the older man. "Aah, you're crazy," laughed the other man.

"You do have him," Rachel persisted. "I know you have. I can prove it."

The blond driver stopped at a junction and turned around to face Rachel. "You're losing your mind. Just focus on your next assignment, and everything will be fine," he ordered menacingly.

Rachel stared. Then she looked down.

She reflected on the paper aeroplane. Had she seen it after all? Was it a paper aeroplane or a falling leaf? Maybe it was a dragonfly or a trick of the light?

She was so tired; she wasn't sure about anything anymore. Tears welled up in her eyes.

KIMBERLEY, the editorial assistant on the Griffton News, considered herself a very spiritual person. She was always keen to see what the stars had in store for her. What was more, she would never date a boy unless she knew his star sign and their signs were compatible with each other.

She had started going to a workshop where she had met her spirit guide, a wonderful young man from the Egyptian era who lived in a place surrounded by sand and pyramids. He was so wise, and they always had adventures together. She could tell him anything at all, and he showed her the most amazing sights. In her spirit, that was.

To tell you the truth, she was honoured when he appeared to her at night the last time because he always gave her such a sense of mental and physical well-being, not to mention a heightened spiritual awareness.

She was just lying in bed, thinking about her day, and he came along, dark and handsome as always.

"Kimberley, my love," he crooned. He wanted her to do something of the utmost importance for him. It was going to help out a friend: Lake Emerson, the guy who carried out research for the other writers.

Kimberley had a huge crush on Lake, as did a lot of the girls in the office, but she doubted Lake had even noticed her. But her spirit guide hinted that Lake might feel the same way about her. Imagine it! The thing he wanted her to do would help Lake out. As a result, it might improve her chances with Lake and even win his heart.

"You're so thoughtful. You know I'd do anything for you," she had told her spirit guide in response.

Then she'd added for good measure, "Of course, if you were alive today, I'd marry you straight away, Samyaza."

THEY DEPOSITED Rachel at the end of Russet Road, on the east side of Griffton, and sped off. The green and gold sports bag was back, a little lumpier and a little heavier than before. They had told her to await orders and not to tell a soul about anything at all. The routine was getting a little predictable.

Rachel was tempted to leave the bag there on the curb and go off down the beach. But she knew that wasn't really an option. She remembered the days when she was free to wander as she pleased. She could walk down to the beach without thinking that anyone was following her. She could go stage diving with Lara down at the Kafka Club, jump into the sea late at night, and know there wouldn't be an assignment waiting for her at the end of it. It seemed like such a long time ago.

What would happen if she wanted to take a holiday? Did she need to tell her new bosses where she was going? What if they said she couldn't go? This was all madness. She was losing her perspective on life.

THEY DEPOSITED

AT HOME, she dragged the bag up the steps and parked it in the corner of her room. She decided she would do her best to ignore it until the time came to deliver it to wherever it needed to be taken.

Tonight, her father was out, but unusually, he had left her a note to tell her there was half a take-away chicken tikka masala in the fridge for her. She went to the fridge, took the curry, plonked herself down, and ate it cold, staring at the wall.

The rest of the evening was uneventful. She checked for messages, had a bath, and played some music. When she eventually went to bed, she slept fitfully, the shadow creatures still trying to enter her mind from the fringes.

The only thing that was different about tonight was that she slept with her curtains closed.

12345

WEDNESDAY MORNING INVADED like a swarm of bees. Rachel shook herself out of an uneasy sleep as the alarm jangled by her ear. She immediately remembered that she had work today.

At lunchtime, she rang the Griffton News and spoke to the editorial assistant, Kimberley. She needed to make sure Lake really was away on holiday, as Kimberley originally told her.

"Griffton News editorial, Kimberley speaking," her voice was light and syrupy.

"Hi, is Lake Emerson there, please?" said Rachel, choosing the direct approach.

"I'm sorry, Lake Emerson isn't available today," sang Kimberley. "Do you know when he'll be back in?"

"I'm sorry, I don't have that information," Kimberley told her, sounding a little nervous.

"This is Rachel Race, and I'm a friend of Lake's. I called yesterday. The thing is, none of his friends can get hold of him. You said yesterday he was on holiday, and Kimberley, I spoke to his family. He's not on holiday."

The line went quiet.

"Okay," whispered Kimberley. "Okay, this is between me and you, right?"

"Of course," said Rachel. She pressed her phone to her ear and waited.

"Lake isn't really on holiday," Kimberley said quietly. Rachel held her breath.

"The paper sent him away on assignment for a few days. He's in Polcombe. He's following up on a lead for one of the other writers, but I can't really talk about it. We do compete with the nationals, you know," preached Kimberley, as though it was an explanation for everything.

"I see," said Rachel. "So why say he's on holiday if he isn't?"

"Look, you can ask him all about it when he comes back," Kimberley told her, and then she added a little too acerbically, "thanks for calling the Griffton News."

Kimberley cut the line.

WITH LARA LEAVING in exactly a week, Rachel thought she should make an effort to see her. In reality, Rachel was feeling extremely friendless and didn't want to spend the evening on her own. She couldn't bear another night in her room with the shadow creatures and the darkness.

She arrived at the Summers' house, pulling the green sports bag behind her because she didn't want to leave it in her room in case her father found it. If it was, as she suspected, packed full of drugs again, then she really didn't want anyone to have a look inside.

Lara opened the door, paused to look at her, and then threw her arms around her friend's neck.

"Oh, Racoon, I thought you'd forgotten about me. I'm not sure whether to let you in or…"

"Move out of the way, loser," bossed Rachel. "You're making me cry."

As Rachel wandered into the house, she noticed how bare it was now. Most of the Summer family's possessions had been packed up and put into boxes that lined the front room walls. Some of the boxes were massive and looked as though they contained things like fridges and cookers. Others were much smaller and could only have contained a dozen or so books or ornaments. All the boxes had big white labels on them, with instructions describing which room their contents belonged in.

Gary and Joel Summer had enjoyed sealing the boxes with

heavy-duty tape, Rachel learned. They also had fun drawing faces on some of them, knowing that some weeks down the line, they would see them again. But meanwhile, they would give the movers a laugh.

The plan was to finish packing by the end of the week when the removal company would come and take everything to the ship. It would take a month and a half for the boxes to get to their new house in California, and while that happened, they would have to live out of their suitcases.

For Lara, this created all sorts of dilemmas for clothes, music, and books. She had all her music on her phone, but what about her clothes? If the ship went down in the middle of the Atlantic, well, that would be: "like, so bad," said Lara.

"Lara Summer, you're not going to lose all your stuff in the middle of the ocean. Stop being such a fool," snapped Rachel.

"Shut up!" countered Lara.

THEY SPENT AN ENJOYABLE EVENING TOGETHER, Lara and Rachel, joking and jousting as much as they ever had and playing their favourite tunes from the past. It was a celebration of their friendship, a best of Racoon and Lemur.

Rachel managed to explain away the bag, saying she'd just been to the gym and hadn't gone home to drop the bag. Lara seemed to go for it because why lie about something like that? Rachel was angst-ridden about lying to her best friend, but her new life was drawing her into a web of concealment and half-truths by the day.

When Lara tried to wheedle out of her any juicy information about what she had been up to, Rachel found herself deflecting every question with vague and unsatisfactory generalities. It was clear Lara suspected something was up because you can't kid your best friend, no matter how hard you try. But she hoped that Lara assumed she was just upset about her moving away. As an explanation, that was far more palatable than the truth.

They established that no one had seen Lake. Rachel told Lara about his supposed assignment in Polcombe, and Lara seemed excited for him.

So, was he really in Polcombe? That girl, Kimberley, said he was. But she also said Lake was on holiday, so something wasn't adding up. It was the only black cloud in the whole wide blue sky of fun they had that evening.

When it came to sleeping, and Lara hit the sack, it seemed natural that Rachel would curl up on her sofa bed across the room so the two could carry on talking. It was so good not to have to be alone. The incident at Lower Ledge Crossing, with the house, the men, and the monsters, all receded to a dreamy distance like it had never happened.

*1*2345

RACHEL FELT Lara shaking her awake and uttered a sleepy, "Hmm?"

"It sounded like it was ticking – I mean, it isn't now. But it was. I'm sure it was. I didn't mean to look, Rachel. But my goodness – what is it?" Lara was saying.

"What's what?" murmured Rachel, pushing back the dream she had been living in for who knows how long. She had been walking on a high mountain path with views of a capacious valley edged with slim fir trees. The mountains were embroidered with white snow, and a cold wind chafed her bare face.

"A bomb? Is it a bomb? Why would you bring a bomb here?" chattered Lara frantically.

"Lemur, don't be so silly," murmured Rachel slowly, pushing herself up on one elbow on the sofa bed.

"What have you got yourself into, Rachel?" Lara was saying. Rachel tried to ignore her. She craned her neck to look over at the bag.

148

The mouth of the green and gold sports bag was open. Inside, she could see a strange bulky object. It had a rectangular metal box at the top and a set of tubes bound with thick silver tape. The tubes had a bundle of red, blue, and black wires snaking out around the side of the object.

Rachel closed her eyes.

CHAPTER 19

"I can't believe you brought that thing into my house," cried Lara, her arms folded. "Is it a bomb?" she added.

Rachel stared at it and remained silent.

"What are you going to do with it?" asked Lara. Rachel bit her lip and tried to keep calm.

"It's not mine," she blurted. "Not buying," stated Lara.

The bedside lamp was on, and Rachel could see the muscles around her friend's mouth twitching.

"Okay, I don't know what it is. I guess I'm just looking after it for some guys," explained Rachel.

"What guys?" Lara demanded.

"I can't tell you. I'm really sorry," said Rachel, sheepishly. "What are you going to blow up?" added Lara.

"I'm not going to blow anything up! Like I said, I'm looking after it for some guys. I don't even know them, but it's, like, a favour."

"Are you insane?" replied Lara.

Rachel stared at the bag. The coloured wires were poking out of the top of the strange box. Was it a bomb? She didn't know.

"I don't think it's a bomb," she said. "It's probably some sort of computer."

"A computer," Lara repeated. She nodded, preferring to believe this explanation. "What sort of computer do you think it is?" she added.

"Maybe it's, like, an engineering computer or something," Rachel suggested.

Amazingly, they had managed to keep their voices down after the initial outbursts, and not woken up Joel and Mr and Mrs Summer.

"I really want to believe you, Racoon, but since that stuff with the knife – your dad chasing you down the road with that knife and your finger, you've been so, like, weird," complained Lara.

Rachel tried to think of something funny to say, like: "I've always been weird," but she just looked at her friend.

"I mean, where do you go?" asked Lara. "When?"

"I don't know. Whenever. This past week. We used to talk all the time. But you just disappeared that night, and you never told me what happened. I can't reach you on your mobile. Then you didn't tell me about Lake Emerson in the library. I mean, what's with that? All the secrecy?"

"I don't know what you're talking about. I work sometimes. I eat sometimes, and I sleep sometimes," said Rachel, poker-faced.

"What about this thing you're looking after for these 'guys'?"

"Look. You're going to have to trust me. I really can't talk about it."

Lara stared at Rachel for some moments.

"I just want my best friend back," she implored.

Then she added, "Now, I need to wash my face, and then we'll, like, figure something out about how you're going to get rid of this thing. Honestly, your 'guys' could have at least told you what it was instead of expecting you to drag it around for them." Lara went to the bathroom, shaking her head.

Rachel waited for her for a few moments.

She quietly debated her next move. Don't tell a soul. Technically, she hadn't told Lara about anything significant, apart from the thing about looking after the bag for some 'guys.' She hadn't told Lara who they were or where they were based. She hadn't told her anything about their intentions because she didn't actually know what they were up to.

She wouldn't really know how to explain all the strange stuff because she barely understood it herself. So, there was no way they could harm Lake or do anything else horrible to her because she hadn't told anyone anything at all. She hadn't told a soul.

Very quietly, Rachel got up from the sofa bed and lifted up her cardigan. She grabbed the handles of the heavy green sports bag and pulled it up towards her body, holding it in both arms.

Then she crept out of Lara's bedroom, down the stairs, and walked out of the house, closing the door quietly behind her. Lara came out of the bathroom and stood at her bedroom door.

She stared at the empty sofa bed.

CALEB HAD THOROUGHLY ENJOYED his escape from the Slovakian prison cell. It always thrilled his soul to see the Dunamis at work, and this adventure had been no exception. The joy of seeing the bars splinter and being able to jump out of the window and escape the Dream Fighters made the injuries he had sustained inconsequential.

He ran across the forest, feeling the cool wind on his face, and savoured his freedom again. He had no doubt the creator would send the Dunamis to heal Jorge's son, whom he had known, 'in the spirit,' was on the verge of death.

What Jorge did, from then on, was his choice. He could choose to serve Samyaza until the end of his days, but that would be the wrong decision. It always is. On the other hand, he could decide to seek the one who had healed his son. The one called the Rescuer. That decision would lead Jorge to freedom from the evil one who held his soul captive. "Decisions, decisions," thought Caleb. "Why are they sometimes so hard?"

Caleb was presently travelling through northern Romania. He hiked through green fields and hills under a dishwater-grey sky and breathed in the musky smell of wet mud.

As he approached the gypsy village, he disturbed a huge flock of white geese. They were paddling in a large puddle and let out short bursts of noise as they flapped their wings. But as he passed, they gathered again at the side of the pool, near the long tufty grass and ridges of mud churned up by the carts.

The Dunamis, filled with compassion, had directed Caleb to one of the poorest gypsy villages in Romania, drawn by the desperate poverty. He instructed him to dwell for a little time with the people, eating their food, hearing their tales, and healing their sick.

Soon, Caleb was surrounded by a crowd of chattering children. They spied him from a great distance and came running to investigate, with the boldest of them leading the pack.

In no time at all, they were pulling at his clothes, touching his skin, and trying to engage him in conversation. The Dunamis gave him kind words to say, and this delighted the children no end.

They were beautiful children, some with dark hair and some with lighter brown hair. They all had bright, clear eyes and colourful, dirty clothes. His new friends smelt muddy and sandy, and he already loved them dearly.

He walked along with his series of satellites rotating around him and staring at him from every angle. The boldest of the children pointed out various things to him. A kind stranger from another country had been helping them to build a well, because they didn't have any clean water before. He had also worked with them to build mud-brick houses. Many of them lived in makeshift houses made with lots of different materials. But the new houses would stay dry when the weather was wet, said the older boy.

They passed some beautiful dark brown horses on the way to the village. They snorted as the crowd walked past. Caleb commented on them, and the children became almost hysterical. He wondered whether the Dunamis had, rather cheekily, given him a joke to tell the children or certainly something with an amusing twist.

Caleb smiled to himself as he walked.

HE WASN'T REALLY VERY heroic at all when it came down to it, but at least he found out. Lake found himself crying like a baby when they started putting him into various stress positions, engaging first his arms, then his legs, and finally his back. It was very painful indeed. He learned some new techniques, though, if he should ever need to inflict some sort of sadistic pain on anyone.

When the young man with short blonde hair finally answered his pleas about why they were doing this to him, he ascertained that firstly, they were sadists who enjoyed inflicting pain but didn't want to leave any marks or break any bones. Secondly, they wanted to scare him enough that he didn't get any more ideas about escaping.

It came as a relief when the nasty sadist decided he had enjoyed himself enough with his judo moves, and it was time to pop his victim back into his room.

So, now Lake was back in the storeroom on the far side of the house, which was full of heavy wooden boxes, most of which were impossible to budge. He sat on the edge of one, clutching his ribs and rubbing his back, feeling sorry for himself.

He found being in this building very disorienting and was no longer able to keep track of time or what day of the week it was. He wanted more than anything to be at home with his mum and dad and wondered when the police would arrive and spring him out. That would be very welcome, but probably wasn't going to happen anytime soon.

He fell back into passing the time, trying to remember adventures from the past, any jokes he could, and any trivial facts that would keep the fear from his mind. It was a tough call this time because he was pretty sure he was going to die at the hands of these men.

Then Lake thought he saw a large shape at the base of the boxes on the opposite side of the room. He instinctively pulled his legs up. He spotted another shape.

Rats.

He hastily placed the soles of his feet on the ledge of the crate and then decided to scramble onto the wooden box next to him. This was on top of a larger one.

He stared at the black rodents as they started to mass on the floor below. He saw them twitching their noses and smelled the damp odour of nasty rat fur.

"I hate rats," he lamented, making sure not to let them leave his sight. He covered his nose and mouth with his tee-shirt just in case.

Meanwhile, the rats began to leave their droppings at the base of the boxes on the far side of the storeroom.

12345

AFTER RACHEL LEFT Lara's house, she just walked and walked. It was nighttime, the early hours of the morning, and she was happy Griffton was never totally asleep and that light traffic accompanied her.

Initially, her cardigan only just managed to trap some of her body heat inside it. But as she walked, she warmed up, and the cold night air no longer touched her. She carried the bag in both arms because it was easier to lug around this way.

She wandered down Ruby Street and along Russet Road, where she lived, but she did not want to go home. Not one bit.

She had that feeling in the pit of her stomach again of being completely isolated and alone.

She passed one pub on Curly Kale Boulevard where a lock-in seemed to be in place. People were drinking even though the place was closed. She could hear laughter and conversation, though the lights at the front were off.

Rachel walked on past.

From the east end of Griffton, she wandered over towards the centre of town. She then got herself onto Roasting Vale Lane, which linked up north and south Griffton.

Staying on Roasting Vale Lane, she crossed Pebble Road and Stony Bridge Road, and Phoenix and Falcon Lanes. She paused at the traffic lights to put the bag down, even though the traffic was more or less dead.

She passed Pomeroy Avenue and Broad Path and eventually came to Deadwood and Driftwood, near the mass of little lanes.

By now, she was closer to the beach road, which ran east to west along the sea. She found herself having to stop more frequently because of the weight of the sports bag. She was no longer speculating about what was in it but was now dragging it along as though it had always been hers.

She walked along the path that led down to the sea, descending the stone steps and fixing her eyes on the beautiful, rolling waves directly in front of her. Although it was dark, the streetlights and the buildings along the south of the city managed to cast enough light for her to see her way down to the beach. She could see people spilling out of the nightclubs and chatting in doorways. It must have gone two o'clock.

There were people up on the beach road, but there was no one around on the beach. She walked in relative silence down along the path that led to the water, enjoying the roar and hiss of the sea.

Finally, she came to the point where she often sat. It was a solitary bench with its back to a wall that acted as a windbreak. Exhausted, she placed the green and gold sports bag by her feet and sat staring at the sea. If it was a bomb and exploded right now, then she would not be bothered one bit.

She zipped her cardigan all the way to the top and folded her arms. Despite feeling alone, she was glad she had found a solitary place where she could get her head together. She closed her eyes, dropped her head, and tried to piece everything together.

She heard men's voices further along the beach growing louder. Rachel let out an exasperated breath.

As they came nearer, she saw that it was a group of four Zodiacs. The last time she met a group of these lads was when they had stopped the train she was travelling on. She'd almost been late for the pickup because of them. They were nothing but trouble.

The Zodiacs all wore black hooded tops and held bottles of cheap cider. Rachel saw they were heading straight for her.

"Oh great," she said. "Just what I need."

CHAPTER 20

The children accompanied Caleb to their nearby village. It had been a very long walk, but he had enjoyed their company immensely. He started to see adult gypsies sitting and chatting with each other. When they spotted him hiking along with all their children around him, they began to stand up and stare. They were trying to assess whether he posed a threat or not. Some of them fidgeted with their clothes, aware a stranger was entering their midst, which generally meant bad news.

But after a while, he won their confidence because of his graceful nature and gentleness and the fact he had handed out a huge number of wooden beads to the children.

He stood for as long as it took, chatting to the men about the things he had seen on his journey and asking them a few general questions, with the Dunamis equipping him to speak the language.

When they finally felt comfortable with him, they decided they wanted to welcome him properly. They had the women make a simple meal of bread and soup with chicken and vegetable pieces in it. He made it clear he was thankful. Perhaps the meal was a luxury for them and a gift to honour him.

He found himself sitting on the mud floor in the dwelling of their leader, who told him about some of the things they had recently made or been given and some of the things they really needed. The leader, who wore an old black fedora, was very candid, and Caleb quietly asked the Dunamis to help them out however he decided to.

Later on, the fedora-wearing leader introduced Caleb to several people in their community who were sick and dying, including a young mother whose childbirth had taken her to the edge of death. They had no money to get her to the hospital, not that the hospital would treat her properly anyway. Being a Gypsy, she just wasn't considered top priority.

Caleb smiled and had compassion for those who were sick, and he asked the Dunamis to heal them, which he did.

One of them was an old woman who had been bedridden for three years. She had been extremely active in the community, and a support to many, but her illness had made her lose hope and waste away. Caleb met her at what could easily have been her lowest ebb, and her face was turned to the wall.

When she was healed, it caused a sensation. Caleb told them he was really nothing special, but his power came from the one who had sent the Dunamis. The Dunamis himself was good and pure and had the power to heal. All Caleb did was follow his lead in obedience. He told them more things that would help them live life to the full. Many of them believed what he told them, but many of them were greatly suspicious and wanted him to go.

Then, like the wind, which changes direction in a split second, the Dunamis instructed Caleb to leave the village and make his way to France, where his next assignment lay.

Caleb was used to being directed daily, with some assignments being short and others long. But all of them were steps on the path to getting to know the Dunamis more intimately. He packed up his backpack, said his goodbyes, and left with a cloud of children buzzing around him.

He hitchhiked to Budapest, then west to Austria, over to Switzerland, and up to Strasbourg, having countless adventures along the way.

Finally, he was in Alsace, France, wandering along a beautiful canal and surrounded by splendid trees and colourful houses.

"Dunamis," he said. "When are you going to take me to meet this Rachel Race?"

The audible inward voice spoke to his spirit and said, "At the appointed time."

"Of course," replied Caleb. "Lead on."

"HEY BABY," droned one of the Zodiacs with a grin and a snarl. He weaved a little as he approached her. She could see he had been drinking. He was still holding a dark bottle.

Rachel pulled her cardigan tighter around herself and watched them closely. They spanned out, trying to surround and intimidate her as she sat on the bench by the sea.

They had all been drinking heavily, which was never good news when it came to Zodiacs. They were prone to acts of extreme violence, destruction, arson, and personal attacks, spurred on by their disaffection and general hatred of society. She knew all about them and what they were about.

She was still unhappy about the antics of their fellow gangsters on the train. Their stupidity had almost made her dangerously late for her assignment to pick up the green bag from Lupus Street Chemist. Now, she was tired and cold, fed up, and definitely not scared of a bunch of boys in black who modelled themselves on hard men from the movies but deep down held a burning hatred for their fathers for abandoning them.

"Are you ready to die?" she shouted at them, startling them with the sound of her voice. "Look in the bag. Go on, I dare you," she added, still maintaining a huge level of volume in her voice.

The tall Zodiac who had hailed her was taken aback but laughed nervously to cover the fact he had lost his edge. He nodded to one of his friends to check out the bag. A Zodiac moved gingerly towards the green bag.

"Don't be such a baby. Open the bag," teased Rachel. She still sat with her cardigan pulled tightly around her, but not because she was fearful. She scowled at the sea.

"Why, what's in there?" asked the Zodiac Kid, trying to sound hard.

"Open the bag," she shouted, making him flinch. As he unzipped the bag, his eyes widened.

"What is it, Too Bad-Man?" called the first Zodiac.

"This, my friends, is a bomb," said Rachel quietly. "And this is where it all ends. Right here, right now," she added, raising her voice again. "Are you ready to die? Because I am!" she shouted, reaching top volume again.

"She's crazy," gulped the one who went by the name of Too Bad- Man. The others were already edging away. Rachel pulled a ball-point pen out of her pocket and clutched it tightly in the air with its tip down.

"The detonator," she explained.

She pushed down the top of the pen with her thumb, making an audible single-click sound.

"You," she ordered, staring directly at Too Bad-Man. "Take off your top and leave it beside me. The rest of you can all go." The other three backed away fast. One of them dropped his cider, which frothed and seeped into the sand. Then they scattered, sprinting away in two directions along the beach.

Too Bad-Man hastily pulled his black hooded top over his head and dumped it down. Suddenly, he had changed from being a macho man to a very young boy, scared of dying.

"Now get out of here," screamed Rachel.

As she watched his back receding and his little legs going up and down as he raced away down the beach, she released the pen.

It clicked a second time as the tip came out and stayed out. Then she clicked it again, watched it retract, and popped it back into her pocket.

"The detonator, I was going to say, isn't in this ball point pen," she said to herself. "I don't know where it is."

Then she laughed uncontrollably for a long time, continuing to giggle as the sun started to make an appearance over to her left.

❧ 12345 ❧

SOMETIME AFTER SIX in the morning, Rachel woke up on her favourite bench by the sea, realising she had managed to doze for a few hours. She was wearing the hooded top.

She immediately noticed the green and gold bag was still by her feet and that, sadly, no one had stolen it. She had dreamed about the bag, that it was shackled to her wrist like a heavy anchor, pulling her down into a dark spirit world where creatures with knife-sharp teeth dwelt.

She looked over the pebbles and sand to the sea and saw the tide was out. She enjoyed the smell of the sea, breathing it in deeply. It poured life into her through her nostrils. Seagulls rose and fell on the moist sand, spotting breakfast amidst the golden grooves. A smoky sun promised a warm and bright day, sending a golden glow across the beach. However, Rachel was cold and in need of some food.

"Ramshack Café," said Rachel, fully aware she was talking to herself. "Time for my next assignment," she giggled. She was also fully aware her response was completely off-beam. Something inside her was starting to kick back. Or break. She didn't know which it was.

She leapt off the bench, grabbed the green bag, and shouted, "Bang!"

12345

LARA SAT IN HER PYJAMAS, her knees up to her chest, on the front room sofa. She had a mug of tea next to her, which was cooling.

Much of the furniture had been packed away, but Gary and Cecilia Summer had decided they needed to keep some comfortable seating. After all, they were going to be living there for a few more days.

Lara's father, Gary, walked into the front room, dressed in his dressing gown and carrying a hot mug of coffee. It was a clever invention that combined a plastic mug and a cafetière, which Lara had given him for Father's Day earlier in the year. She loved the way he used it every day.

"Is Rachel coming down for breakfast, or is she going to sleep in?" Gary asked.

"Rachel's gone, dad," said Lara quietly.

"I suppose she had to go to work? I don't envy her," smiled Gary.

Lara stayed quiet.

"Did you girls have a good evening?" he asked, sitting down on the sofa next to her.

Lara fought an internal battle, trying to answer this simple question.

"Yeah, we had a great time. It was just like the old days," she said hastily. Then she added, "Is mum up yet?"

"No, she's going to stay in bed for a while. Why do you ask?" said her dad, raising his eyebrows. He knew his daughter well enough to know that she wanted to tell him something. So, he bided his time and sipped his coffee. He knew her so well that she would come to him to talk, whereas Joel would rather go to Cecilia if he needed to talk.

And then it came. "I'm a bit worried about Rachel," Lara quietly informed him.

"Okay, I've heard this one before," thought Gary, but he indicated to Lara to continue.

"Why don't you start from the beginning?" he said calmly.

It was a normal Thursday morning in a normal week, and Daniel William Harcourt woke up at five thirty in his seven-bedroom mansion on the edge of Griffton, as he always did. Arabella, his wife, woke slightly to murmur a good morning to him. Then she went back to sleep as she always did. Daniel went to wash his face in his bedroom sink and then opened a curtain.

Before long, he showered and wore a silk dressing gown, deep red and blue in colour. He stood and fiddled with the cord, trying to get it just right.

At around six o'clock, he stood in the large red and golden bedroom, which had a view of a terraced garden with a croquet lawn and the long drive leading up to a pair of wrought-iron gates. Daniel looked around his room, seeing his darling Arabella asleep under the silk sheets, his favourite sofa by the other window, and his shelf of bedtime reading books. He looked at the trophy he had been awarded for hunting and his favourite tweed deerstalker hat, which was resting on the top corner of a wooden chair.

Then he made his way to the next room, his dressing room, where he dressed distractedly, selecting a Ralph Lauren shirt, Hugo Boss slacks, an Armani sports jacket, and Gucci slip-ons.

Focusing more, he took out a large overnight bag and packed it full of clothes and toiletries. He took it out of the bedroom and along the corridor to his office and gathered up his passport and some papers. These he placed in a leather backpack along with the book he was part way through. He grabbed his gold phone, reached for his leather wallet, and whisked his bags down to the front door.

Making a final circuit of the house, Daniel kissed his wife on the forehead and placed an envelope on her bedside table, then went to kiss the boys, Cameron and Rory.

On Cameron's table, he placed two rings, one of them gold and the other platinum. He took off his Breitling watch and placed it quietly on Rory's table. They would find out about the trust funds in good time.

Down in the hall, Daniel snatched up his car keys, which were on the dark wooden table by the grandfather clock. He lifted up his bags, one in each hand, and left the house for the last time without looking back.

CHAPTER 21

Rachel was ravenous. She gobbled up her eggs, sausages, bacon, fried slices, hash browns, tomatoes, and mushrooms and then ordered more toast. The hot tea revived her, pouring life back into her veins.

"Mo, this is great," she called out to her waitress friend, who was reading a newspaper on the counter. Mo looked up lazily and smiled.

It hadn't even been a whole week since she was here in Ramshack Café, on the beach. It was the morning after her encounter with the lights on Griffton Cliff. Her mother's face in the lights. It had been the start of this strange rollercoaster adventure. Lupus Street Chemist. Lower Ledge Crossing again. The kidnappers.

The lights on the cliff could have been the beginning of it all. Or perhaps losing the finger and being chased around Griffton General Hospital by a big black cat had been the start. Yes, that was more likely, she thought. Whichever way it was, the events had surrounded and smothered her, and she knew she was no longer in control of her own future. If she ever had been.

After all, how much say do we actually have about when the big things happen, like illness, injury, or death? Her mother dying had not been her choice, but it happened. That was a hard lesson in helplessness.

In many ways, she knew all about the ins and outs of being at the mercy of life's circumstances. When her mum died, she went through the whole 'angry at everyone; angry at God' thing. In the end, she had to conclude that bad things happen, and that was the way of the world. As for God, she'd just have to give him a hard time when she met him.

So, assignment one had been a reminder that she wasn't in charge of her life, though she didn't really need reminding of that fact. Assignment two had been to travel to the Lupus Street Chemist in Sandy Bottom Cove. Assignment three had been to deliver the bag to Lower Ledge Crossing on Griffton Cliff. How many more assignments before she qualified? What was she being tested for, anyway?

It was no surprise when the phone in the café rang, and it was for her again.

"This is Rachel. What's next?" she said.

The androgynous voice at the other end of the line spoke in a bored voice. "Your fourth assignment is to take the bag to the Griffton Metropolitan Hotel at one o'clock on Friday afternoon. Go to the hotel restaurant, order some food, then leave the bag under your chair and leave the hotel. That is all. It is imperative to follow these orders exactly and don't tell a soul." The caller hung up.

Mo looked up from her papers enquiringly. "Crank caller," explained Rachel.

❧ 12345 ❧

RACHEL MADE her breakfast last until it was time to go to work. Then she walked along the beach to Rock and Shock, feeling numb.

When she turned up, seconds before opening time, Iona

commented, "You look terrible, like you've spent the night on the street."

Iona was herself immaculately turned out in a floral dress and matching accessories. She had braided her hair and painted her nails to match the outfit. This morning, she smelled of vanilla.

"Leave me alone, Iona," grunted Rachel. Then she added, "I don't suppose you've got any deodorant on you? Maybe some perfume. Something vanilla-scented?"

"Do you know what? I think I've got some in my bag," smiled Iona.

"Great. I think I smell."

"You said it, honey," said Iona airily.

IT WAS a quiet day at the record shop, and Iona and Rachel had the opportunity to chat and play some new tunes at full volume. Ben was up in London, looking for some new stock and making a day of it, so they had the place to themselves for the entire day.

Rachel asked her friend, "Tell me something about yourself that, like, nobody else knows."

"You mean like an annoying habit or something?"

"I don't know. Something weird," said Rachel.

"I don't know what you're trying to say. There's nothing weird about me," laughed Iona.

"Sure."

"Well, I'm a pretty open book. You know me. I like colour, purples, and pinks, orange and red and yellow, preferably all together. I like my houseplants, especially Benny the cactus. I don't know what to say. Do you know about my family? I don't really see much of my parents anymore. Not since I left home," twittered Iona.

"What happened there?" asked Rachel.

"There isn't much to tell. I grew up outside Cambridge, and

it was pretty boring. I'm afraid this isn't very dramatic, really. They're nice people and everything, my folks, but I just found life too dull up there. Nothing ever happened. Then I met Joe, you know all this. I moved down to Griffton. Joe disappeared on me. I got this job and my flat. You really must come round sometime soon, Rachel. We can have dinner and a laugh. Do you even eat?"

"As a matter of fact, I had a full English breakfast this morning," claimed Rachel proudly.

"No kidding," cried Iona, clearly impressed. "Of course, I'm veggie, so I'm not a hundred percent in favour," she joked.

Rachel stared out of the window.

"So, what about you, Rachel? Why don't you tell me something about yourself that I don't know?" asked Iona.

"Well, you know about my mum. You know about my dad. Nothing much to say there. You know about my best friend Lara: that she's going to California in a few days," said Rachel.

"Don't tell a soul," thought Rachel.

"There isn't really too much else to say," she concluded. "Have you got any plans for lunch?"

❦ 12345 ❦

IONA DID HAVE some plans for lunch, so Rachel was left to her own devices. She had parked the green bag in a back room, where she normally kept her things. Iona hadn't commented on it. They locked up the place over lunchtime and hung the sign on the door which said: "Gone rocking. Later, dude!" Ben loved the sign. It always made him laugh.

Rachel felt a fantastic relief at leaving the bag behind at the shop. "It's bound to be a bomb," she thought and wondered whether she should call the police and tip them off anonymously while she was out at lunch. But she knew that wasn't really an option. Lake was probably trapped in that house, and she was wasting time when she should have been trying to work out how to rescue him.

The main problem was that this whole thing was so much bigger than she was. It made it hard to think straight, and if she did try to work it all out, it gave her a dull ache in her stomach. As far as she could see, all she had to do was follow the orders, and everything would turn out okay. Of course, she had no guarantee of this.

After lunch, Rachel opened up the shop again. Iona had told her she would be back late as she had to take care of some banking business in town. As she sat at the counter, she answered a call from Lara.

"Hi Rachel, remember me?"

"Don't be silly."

Then they had a very uncomfortable exchange, where Lara basically laid into Rachel for leaving in the middle of the night without saying goodbye. Being selfish and self-centred. Not even having a mobile phone she was contactable on. And, greatest of all, carrying around a live bomb.

"I don't know what you think you're doing, you maniac, and you should, like, give me one good reason why I shouldn't, like, come right over to the shop right now with the police," cried Lara.

"Look, Lara, I don't think it's a bomb," defended Rachel rather feebly, thinking in her heart it was definitely a bomb. "I just have to do this thing. It's, like, a delivery," she added.

"Where to?" demanded Lara.

"I don't know. A hotel," jabbered Rachel without thinking.

"Which hotel?" asked Lara.

"Or maybe a restaurant," said Rachel hastily.

"Are they paying you for this?" asked Lara.

"Err, no, not really," said Rachel.

"Well, they should be," ranted Lara. Then she said, a little more calmly, "Listen, Racoon, I know you can't tell me everything. I'm not, like, stupid. But I was talking to my dad, and he says…"

"You what?" screamed Rachel.

She stared out of the window of the shop, across the beach, and down to the rolling waves. She suddenly realised she had been betrayed and laid bare. Don't tell a soul, they had warned her. Now, everyone knew her business. Lara and her family and probably the authorities. She had been sloppy and stupid, and now she'd have to pay.

"And what does Gary have to say?" Rachel demanded.

Lara confessed quietly, "He thinks you should tell the police. And I agree."

"Oh, you guys have no idea," fumed Rachel and hung up.

LATE IN THE MORNING, the ferry to France was ready for boarding. Daniel had his leather backpack on his back and his overnight bag by his side as he queued to embark. He had spent the morning flipping through the national papers in the boarding lounge, sipping espressos and trying not to catch anyone's gaze.

It seemed like the people making the crossing were business-people like him, couples, a few families with kids, and a handful of single holidaymakers. The sea was quiet, and he expected a fair crossing.

Standing tall on the top deck, he blew a theatrical goodbye kiss to the headland as it receded. The large ferry ploughed inexorably through the sea, churning the water behind it and turning it snow white. It looked cold down there in the waves, thought Daniel.

He enjoyed the feel of the cold breeze through his hair, beating at his face. It felt as though his old life, with all its troubles, was being blown away by the wind.

He was two hours into the six-hour journey from Griffton to

Roscoff in Brittany when Samyaza appeared in his spirit. It was probably inevitable, felt Daniel in a heavy-hearted way.

Samyaza, gnarly and old with a hideous face and dead eyes, considered him coolly and left a stench in his spirit.

"Hello, Samyaza," said Daniel, as the wind gently rubbed his face like sandpaper.

"Daniel. I'm disappointed in you taking leave without my permission. What is the meaning of this?" asked Samyaza in a menacing tone.

"I thought I'd take a little holiday," explained Daniel. "You know, see the countryside, France, Portugal. I don't remember inviting you, though."

"You did that a long time ago, my friend," said Samyaza. "I remember the weak boy who would never have amounted to anything. You and I both know that Arabella was way out of your league and always would be. You were destined to a life of mediocrity, tucked away in some hovel on the east end of Griffton. If it wasn't for me, you would still be crying in the dark over your many failings."

"Oh, leave me alone," implored Daniel.

"But you called on me, and together, we grabbed the world by its throat. You've travelled all over the world. You like your big house in the suburbs and your personal shoppers. I know you do. Do you remember Arabella's face when you fastened that wonderful necklace around her? It was a diamond necklace from the De Beers Classics collection if I remember correctly. You bought it for her to celebrate your first big deal with that Japanese bank."

"Pretty trinkets," Daniel snapped.

"That's not what you said at the time," said Samyaza. "The two of you dined at the top restaurants, eating magnificent game and drinking the best wines on the planet. Remember the 100-point '82 Chateau Lafite? Berry Bros and Rudd guaranteed it and valued it at over three thousand pounds. You and Arabella quaffed it in half an hour with the Foreign Secretary, and that bore from Rothschild."

"Yes, I do remember all of those things, Samyaza. And I also remember all the innocent blood I have on my hands, people I hurt for you."

"No one is innocent. Everyone is culpable for something. Men, women, and children," Samyaza said calmly. "Think of the tiny child who learns to manipulate and rage right from the cradle. As he grows older, he learns to lie and harm in many beautiful ways. He slips with ease into gossip and slander and murderous thoughts. Later, he gains the desire for power and possessions, as well as the lusts of the eyes and the lusts of the flesh. No. No one is innocent," sang Samyaza, licking his lips.

"So you always say. I have done things for you that I would never have done had I not met you. You have turned me into a monster," cursed Daniel. "But the time has come for it to end. I have had enough. Our partnership is finished. The deal's over. There is no way I will work for you anymore. You and I are parting company from this moment."

Daniel spat his thoughts out into the wind, no longer caring about the consequences of resisting his master. He had lived for too long with the illusion he was free of this beast. He had enjoyed the time Samyaza had left him and his family alone. But now he wanted to be truly free for good.

Samyaza was quiet for a while, and Daniel found it hard to make out his shape.

His heart was racing, and he was aware of his breath, which had grown more rapid. He knew he had been here before, all those years ago, when he had faced down the monster and poured out his gall in a solitary place. As a result, Samyaza had disappeared for a number of years, only to reappear to Daniel's dismay.

"Very eloquent," said Samyaza. "But sadly pathetic. I haven't finished with you yet, not by a long chalk."

Daniel felt a tightening around his heart. "What are you doing?" he gasped, putting his hand to his chest.

"You see, my pet, there is no escaping me. You and I are linked forever, spirit to spirit. I go wherever you go. I will never leave you or leave you alone. Not ever. You will never be without your Samyaza."

"So be it," stated Daniel as he vaulted the bars and flung himself overboard from the top of the ferry. He plunged into the icy frothing waters far below.

But just before Daniel hit the water, Samyaza forced a chilling scream from his throat and fled his body, racing off into the spiritual wilderness in search of the next soul to inhabit.

CHAPTER 22

"It's been a very long time since I was in England, my friend," Caleb Noble enthused his travelling companion, Doctor Eli Doctorian. He was saying it for perhaps the sixth time.

Caleb grinned like a little boy. His round black sunglasses caught the light of the lunchtime sun over the English Channel. He was clearly excited about going back to England. The land held a special place in his heart, and this much was clear. His fellow traveller smiled back as he expertly steered the large yacht with one muscular arm on the wheel.

Eli was an accomplished sailor who spent most of his life on the water, being a fan of everything from large cruise liners to thirty-foot yachts like this one, which was called the Armenian. He had wavy grey hair and a full beard and was in his early seventies. He cracked jokes as they sailed, remembering funny situations from his many travels across the globe.

Eli's favourite drink was manufactured in Nepal, and Caleb had surprised him by producing a bottle of it for him, which thrilled him to no end. It wasn't really his own initiative, Caleb admitted to his friend. When he was in Chainpur, Nepal, the Dunamis had urged him to buy a bottle, and keep it tucked away in his wash bag. He gave him absolutely no clue that he would run into his old friend again, but that was the Dunamis. He loved to surprise, entertain, and bring joy to people.

As a result, both Caleb and Eli were nearly hysterical when the Dunamis brought them together in northern France and even provided the Nepalese ginger drink to celebrate.

They reminisced about the past and adventures they had shared and had the strange Nepalese drink along with some pita bread and vegetable dips. For Caleb, it was a feast with a dear friend, and it tasted all the better for their friendship, which stretched across the decades. He told the Doctor as much as he could about his current mission. All the while, Eli nodded sagely.

Right now, they were somewhere between France and England, closer to the latter than the former. As he stared at the sea and tried to make out the shoreline of southern England, Caleb entered an open vision. He was experiencing these more and more these days and getting used to the Dunamis pointing things out either in the spirit or the material world. Things that were happening or were about to manifest.

The most recent time was when he was sitting in the Himalayan Mountains, having a coffee. The Dunamis had given him an open vision of the girl, Rachel Race, being pursued by dark forces in the form of a black panther. The vision was like an internal movie of the action as it took place, playing in his head. He had immediately responded and broken the power levelled against her, saving her life, he believed. It was all part of walking in step with the Dunamis, catching the visions, and doing the business. It was a total thrill.

So, when Caleb experienced another open vision there on the waters with his friend Eli, it came as no surprise. In his vision, he saw the man fall into the water. He saw him hit the surface and sink under the cruel waves. He even saw him sink down and die. Then, the vision ended.

As Caleb stared across the water, he saw the channel crossing ferry enter his field of vision to the left and instinctively knew he had to act. He tore off his sunglasses, cast them onto the deck, and plunged into the waters.

The doctor watched dreamily as he steered the boat. Then he efficiently moved to slow the vessel down, his muscles bulging as he ducked under the boom and moved around the deck, working the ropes.

12345

RACHEL TRIED to calm her nerves as she approached the Griffton Metropolitan Hotel. It was half past twelve on Friday. Her drop-off was timetabled for one o'clock in the afternoon at the hotel restaurant.

Thursday night had yielded little sleep for Rachel and had left her nerves jangling. She had spurned the thought of food and instead spent time applying a layer of foundation to her face to mask her tiredness.

She stopped several yards from the hotel and took in the broad and tall building. It was one of Griffton's oldest and largest hotels and part of the Golden Metropolitan Group, which had majestic hotels located in every southern city.

She noted the hallmark flower bowls on either side of the hotel doors: six pairs in total. The wide doors themselves had golden adornments and featured smoked glass panes that bore the hotel's insignia, a stylised GM logo.

There were plenty of people floating about, thought Rachel. It should be easy to blend in and find a place at a table. She was dressed smartly, all in black, with her hair tied back and a pair of elegant black sunglasses to cover her bloodshot eyes.

She set her jaw and walked forward with as much purpose as she could muster. She tried to ignore the heavy green and gold gym bag at the end of her right arm, instead trying to emphasise the dainty black bag around her left. She crooked her left arm and rested her hand, with the stump of the little finger against her handbag as she walked.

An old man in uniform nodded a 'hello' to her as she pushed through the double doors and sleepwalked into the expansive lobby of the hotel. But she clenched her teeth and silently passed by, ignoring him on purpose.

Then she was in the main area of the lobby, a huge, airy hall with marble floors and a reception desk across the room. People reclined on the leather seats and sofas. They were flipping through fashion and lifestyle magazines, drinking coffee, and chatting lightly with one another. Rachel glanced across the lobby. She saw the sign for the restaurant and moved towards it. "So far, so good," she thought.

As she walked, her confidence began to evaporate.

"I am carrying a live bomb," her inner voice told her. The voiceless voice continued relentlessly, "And I am about to kill a lot of people in this hotel."

"No," said Rachel under her breath, "I am carrying out an assignment to deliver this machine. That is all."

"I am about to detonate a bomb in a hotel and kill all the people dining in this fancy restaurant in front of me," said the silent voice inside Rachel's heart, or perhaps it was her guts; she wasn't sure. But it was pretty loud.

"I have to do this," muttered Rachel, "because if I don't do this, they're going to cut off my hand." She stared through the black lenses of her sunglasses, seeing yet another flower arrangement ahead on a table. The table was directly outside the restaurant, and it marked the place where her assignment would end once she'd made the drop and come back out.

"You still have time to run. You don't have to do this," said the ongoing dialogue in Rachel's head.

"And then they're going to kill me, and Lake, and probably Iona, Lara, Ben, Joel, Dad, and all my friends," muttered Rachel, perspiring slightly. She walked upright, eyes trained on the restaurant doors, on target to arrive in seconds at her destination.

As she prepared to push through the doors, a man materialised and spoke to her. She was suddenly aware of all the sounds around her. She heard diners laughing and talking, cutlery chinking, and could also smell the strong aroma of steaks. It was like she had awoken from a long sleep.

"Can I help you, ma'am?" asked the gentleman who had appeared at the doors of the restaurant. He was a lean man with an unreadable face, but his badge revealed that he was the restaurant manager.

Rachel froze, believing the man had indicated somehow that he knew all about the bomb in her sports bag and wanted her to explain herself. She stared at him, her mouth slightly open.

"Perhaps you are wishing to dine here today?" suggested the manager, with a hint of a French accent.

Rachel heard in her head: "Die here today. Perhaps you are wishing to die here today?" She shook off the false voice.

"No. Sorry, yes. Please. It's just me. A table for one, please," stuttered Rachel as she brushed off her sunglasses so as not to appear rude. She tried to look him in the face but glanced away. "He knows," she thought.

"Certainly, ma'am. Just this way," insisted the manager, who led her through the doors into the restaurant and pulled a chair for her at a table near the centre of the restaurant. It looked like they were doing good business today.

The restaurant manager handed her over expertly to her waiter with a few words of introduction and an assurance that the man would look after her. Then he nodded and moved on.

"May I take a room number?" asked the waiter, posing an immediate problem for Rachel.

"Actually, I work in town," she mumbled. "I'm just here for the food," she added superfluously.

"Of course," said the waiter.

"Oh, could you, like, tell me where your ladies' room is? If that's okay?" added Rachel before she sat down.

"Of course," said the waiter. He indicated a door at the back of the room and discreetly disappeared into the kitchens.

Rachel, still holding tightly onto her green and gold bag, fled the table for the safety of the ladies' toilets.

CALEB CRADLED the dead man in his arms as his good friend looked on with a glass of iced tea in his hand. Doctor Doctorian had decided to slow the yacht as much as he was able and throw out a ring there in the middle of the Channel.

In the distance, boats moved to and fro, doing their own thing and minding their own business. Here on the good ship Armenian, it was just the three of them, the two living men and one dead one, in a vast blue-green sea under a cloudy blue sky.

"How long do you think he's been dead?" asked Eli, taking a sip of his drink and watching the dripping figures before him.

"Hard to tell. Minutes? Half an hour, maybe? You know it doesn't matter," mourned Caleb. He had tears in his eyes for the dead man who looked from his clothing as though he was accustomed to wealth. He was a handsome man in his late forties, with thinning hair and lines around his eyes. "I wonder who he is," whispered Caleb.

"Aren't you going to wake him up?" asked Eli, a smile playing about his lips.

"You know that's down to the Dunamis and the strength of our faith," said Caleb, regarding his friend with a frosty but kind glare.

"Okay, I'll put down my drink then."

Caleb waited for his friend to get ready, closed his eyes, and then called on the mercy and power of the Dunamis to do his work. Eli did the same. They pressed into the Dunamis, feeling his love and power rising. Then they waited. It was as simple as that.

Daniel William Harcourt opened his eyes.

AT AROUND TWELVE FORTY-FIVE, Rachel had sufficiently composed herself in the ladies' toilets. She returned to her table at the centre of the restaurant, dragging the bag behind her. It was heavy and bulky, and she wished she had never set eyes on it on the counter in Lupus Street Chemist. She hated it with a passion.

She should have taken notice when she saw the legs of the dead man by the counter. He had been dead and not sleeping or unconscious, she was sure. "These people don't make mistakes, and that man was certainly dead," thought Rachel.

Then, there was that man who emerged from the back of the chemist. The one who worked for Samyaza, whoever Samyaza was. "But he was far too smooth and calm, so did he really?" she wondered.

"We're all slaves to him. No one's free. You'd better start getting used to it," he had said to her. What did that mean?

"Well, I guess it means this," she said to herself as she pretended to look at the menu.

She was having a hard time focusing her eyes to actually read the menu, but at the same time, she was hyper-aware of her surroundings. She was aware of every person at every table around her. She knew what they were wearing and what they were saying. The tables were full now, around forty or so beautifully presented dining tables, which meant the diners numbered over a hundred people.

"All I need to do is order some food, leave the bag under the chair, and leave the hotel," Rachel told herself.

A coldness came over her, and she sat up straight in her chair. "Mum's dead. She's not coming back. Dad will never be there for me. Lara's gone. My life is meaningless, and I no longer want to live. And these people? No one is innocent," Rachel said to herself as she ran her finger down the list of entrees.

The waiter appeared at her side. "Can I take your order, miss?" he asked politely.

Rachel's stream of thought continued. "No one is innocent. Bad things happen to good people. I just have to do this one thing, leave the bomb and slip away. Then, I get to keep my hand. And Lake lives."

She carried on, "It's my hand anyway, and I like my hand. Besides, if I was one of these people here, who'd care about me anyway? If your number's up, your number's up. And, you know, it's not like I'm actually pushing the button or anything. I'm just leaving a package, that's all. Someone's probably going to come in and pick it up after I've gone. What do I know?"

The waiter spoke again. "Erm, what?" said Rachel.

"Are you ready to order, miss?" he asked for the third time. "Sorry," replied Rachel. She glazed over as she looked at the menu. "I'd like that one and that one," she burbled.

"And to drink?"

"Er," said Rachel. She felt very uncomfortable.

"Sorry?"

"A ginger beer?" she asked.

"We have ginger ale," he replied. Rachel nodded her assent.

As the waiter went to the kitchen to relate the order, Rachel prepared to exit the hotel swiftly, leaving the bag under her seat.

What she would do after that, she hadn't decided. But she was certain it would be the end for her one way or another.

The main thing was to walk quickly and then run for her life.

CHAPTER 23

"You've certainly been through a lot, young Daniel Harcourt," said Eli to his new boat guest.

They had managed to dry the man out and place a drink in his hand to help him recover from his death experience. Daniel wore a large blue bathrobe and felt totally surreal, staring at the two men whom he assumed were angels.

"Now we know your story, how Samyaza got hold of you and put you through your paces and all. I know Eli here would agree that there's something you ought to do pretty quickly, which is to claim your freedom," explained Caleb in a measured fashion.

"Now, this is just our suggestion, and it is entirely up to you. But we reckon you have been spared for a purpose. You also don't want that Samyaza fellow to come back, do you?" he asked.

Daniel shook his head.

"In which case, it is wise to fill the void that Samyaza left, you see?" continued Caleb. "There is a creator, and he knows you, and he loves you, though you don't know him yet. He rescues and makes people new again. You can know him from now on, if you want. That old stuff that Samyaza led you to do is all in the past now. You can decide to walk away from it."

Daniel nodded, so Caleb continued. "This decision will give you freedom and power. It will keep Samyaza coming back when he finds out you're still walking the earth. And believe me, he will try to come back when he finds out you've tricked him. But like we say, the choice is yours."

Then he explained to Daniel about the Rescuer and his Dunamis, about the cost involved in following him, but also about his raw power and the pure thrill of his presence.

They left Daniel to reflect on the possibility of a new life, but he didn't need much time. With many tears and the desperation of a drowning man reaching for the rope, Daniel grabbed hold of the lifeline and met the Dunamis for the first time.

Caleb and Eli sat on the deck in awe, watching his face glow as the Dunamis breathed new life into him.

As her drink came, Rachel realised she had no appetite and no desire to drink anything. She had one thing in mind: the thing she had to do, which was to carry out assignment number four. She had already decided the hard part was over. That was to bring the bag into the hotel and place it under a restaurant table. Job done.

The easy part now remained. That was to slip away out of the door and disappear in Griffton's complex street system. What happened after that was none of her business.

She watched the waiter move to the other side of the restaurant and took a deep breath.

As she looked over to the door, she saw two police officers entering the restaurant. They were clearly two of Griffton's finest, tall and confident and wearing the blue uniform. They had their helmets under their arms.

They scanned the room, and Rachel instinctively bowed her head, already acting like a criminal. Their silver and blue

Griffton police badge glinted as they moved towards the counter, probably in search of the restaurant manager.

Then, it came to her quickly, like a dagger in her flesh. Lara had betrayed her. Her best friend Lara and Lara's well-meaning father Gary had tipped off the police. Now, they were hunting for Rachel.

"Time to run," she thought.

She watched the policemen move over to the far end of the massive restaurant and waited for a few moments. For the time being, she was safe amongst so many diners. But it had been a mistake to pause and look around because she saw the faces of the unwary people.

A couple, clearly in love, gazed and smiled at each other at one table. At another, a young family ate dessert, their baby boy giggling and smearing yoghurt across his cheeks. People talked business at other tables while sipping wine and fluttering their fingers.

In a moment of madness, Rachel felt herself lean down and grab for the bag under the table, feeling for the leather straps with her right hand. She carried it up to her lap, clasping her left hand over it. Then she pushed herself back in her chair and walked hurriedly to the exit, hugging the sports bag close to her body. She was clenching her teeth as she went.

She didn't see if the police had noticed her leave but made sure her head was down as she crossed the hotel lobby.

She passed the huge, beautiful flower arrangements and the corridors that led off to hidden hotel rooms. She flipped her sunglasses down over her eyes as she sped further into the lobby with its high ceiling and marble floors.

Walking quickly, she passed the sofas and the reception desk and left the building through the front doors, ignoring everyone around her. She passed the old man in uniform at the door but was blind to him this time.

Tears started to flow as she carried the heavy burden out of the hotel and onto the street, but she propelled herself away from the hotel building and across the road.

As she got to the other side, she started to shake with adrenaline and emotion. She wanted to drop the bag but felt it had become an extension of her body now.

A car door opened close by, and a man got out.

It was the man with short-cropped blonde hair and the long scar down his face. He was scowling. As he came close, she found herself unable to move.

"It's you," she mouthed, but no words came.

"You are so weak," he spat at her. She blinked. The man pulled the green and gold sports bag out of her arms. Then he turned and sprinted with it towards the hotel.

"No!" shouted Rachel, her eyes wide. But again, no words came out.

The man wove his way between the cars and approached the hotel at a trot that turned into a walk. Next, he was inside.

Someone bundled her into the back of the waiting car, bruising her thigh as she caught it on the door. There was a man beside her and a man in the driving seat. "This is game over," she thought.

The rest of the events had a dreamlike quality about them. She tried the door handle and learned that the child lock was on, found herself restrained by a large man in the seat next to her, felt the car merge with the traffic, and saw the Griffton Metropolitan Hotel exploding from out of the back window.

The grand building just seemed to crumple as the high ceilings slumped down onto the ground floor. The sound of the explosion was both crisp and muted. The car drove on through Griffton's maze of streets.

She closed her eyes but could still imagine the sounds of screaming.

Over the next few days, Rachel lived in a continual state of shock and denial.

Haunted by the Griffton Metropolitan Hotel bombing, she endured long hours of silent horror. Between those, she managed to clutch small handfuls of sleep in her room. Her body had been close to collapse as it was, having endured a week of sleeplessness, so slumber was most welcome.

There was a relatively comfortable bed, and they fed her regularly, which was a bonus. But still, the horror gnawed at her mind. She thought of the people in the restaurant. No one deserved to die like that. Not really. But maybe they didn't. Perhaps it never happened.

Alongside the shock of the explosion was the experience of being confined, and this lasted several days through what must have been the weekend. Rachel scurried around her room like a gerbil in a wheel or lay on the bed and cried. From time to time, she reasoned that if she had been arrested by the police rather than swiped by these psychopaths, then she'd probably be in a cell somewhere else.

Desperation weighed her down.

The room smelled salty and dank but had a flushable toilet in a connected cubicle. She had room to pace, and they had given her a table and some writing equipment, but she had no desire to write anything.

Of course, she tried the door many times and even attempted to prise off the vent above the bed and lift the carpet to see if there was a hatch or something under there. But she was well and truly imprisoned.

Besides the bombing and the confinement, the other thing that gripped her and refused to depart was the fear of the monster that would come and take her hand. Would they use a blade? Would it hurt? Naturally, she knew it would.

To begin with, anyone who approached her room made her jump, thinking that this was the moment. She became used to the idea that she was going to take the punishment because she hadn't completed her mission. It was a strange way of thinking. She knew that. Only, she felt as though she was the one who had messed up. She was the one who was 'weak,' as that man had said.

The assignment itself had been so simple, yet so hard when it came down to it. All she had to do was take a bag into a hotel and walk out, but she couldn't do it. When it came down to it, she just wasn't a killer. Now, she had to wait for her punishment.

She frequently thought about the people left in the carnage of the exploded building: the wounded and the dead.

"God help me," she simply said, over and over again.

LAKE WAS glad to see the rats were gone. He had hated the sight of them gnawing around the edges of whichever crate he was perched on. He hated their stench.

He quickly grew tired of living on top of the crates, which he had been forced to do for the best part of a day. Now, he was regularly being allowed to go to the toilet down the hall rather than being forced to hold on until it hurt. He was even allowed to have a wash, which was great because he was used to having a shower every day and was finding it incredibly hard to stay unwashed.

Along with the disappearance of the rats, he had also noticed something different about his captors, this strange cult of wizards. It was almost as if they had lost their confidence. Instead of striding purposefully about the house, they now shuffled around as though they were passing the time. He also noticed the chanting had grown louder and more desperate.

"Something's up," he said to himself.

THE GROUP of occultists was growing more desperate to try to reach Samyaza through whatever means they could. The boss man, Daniel Harcourt, who had a direct line to Samyaza, was missing in action. And no matter how hard they chanted and divined, the cloud of the presence refused to descend for them.

Having exhausted their arsenal of spells and incantations and animal sacrifices, their thoughts were now turning to human sacrifice. They held two candidates in the house for this purpose: the girl and the reporter. Daniel had said not to harm the boy, but perhaps things had changed now. Perhaps what Samyaza really wanted was more blood.

It was possible that the hotel bombing wasn't enough. Could it be that Samyaza wanted to see the extent of their commitment to him before he came and instructed them further? They knew from experience that Samyaza demanded results. All they had to do now was act, surely.

<h1 style="text-align:center">CHAPTER 24</h1>

An announcement came over the airport loudspeaker for the remaining passengers for flight BA269 to Los Angeles to go to the gate. Three members of the Summer family were already there: Gary, Cecilia, and Joel. The terminal was packed as people left for their summer holidays.

Lara stared at the magazine racks in a daze and thought about Rachel. She was dressed in jeans and a long figure-hugging black shirt with a short cardigan over the top, a cardigan Rachel had given her for her last birthday. "A present from Rachel Racoon," she had thought sadly when she put it on this morning.

She was bitterly disappointed Rachel hadn't been around to say goodbye properly. When she thought about it, her emotions caught in her throat and tried to choke her. She had finished packing her hand luggage and then called her, said an emotional goodbye to the rest of the gang, and called her again. Then she waited for the taxi to the train station and called her yet again. Landline. Mobile. Work phone, just in case. She just couldn't get hold of Rachel Race.

Her family made sympathetic noises, but their heads were already in America. Joel had muttered something about not being able to get hold of Lake, but guys being guys, he didn't seem to care that much.

So, as usual, Rachel wasn't answering her phone or replying to the texts. What was more, her dad was just as bad. He was distinctly rude when she asked where her friend was. He was very grumpy, saying, "How on earth should I know? She's a grown girl. She can look after herself."

As for Rachel, she had been engulfed in this new life of secrecy and intrigue, and there didn't seem to be a way in for Lara. But being a loyal friend, she thought, Lara had not involved herself or called the police as she should have done. Maybe she should have. If Rachel had anything to do with last Friday's hotel bombing at the Griffton Metropolitan, then she had important information that could have stopped it.

As it was, an international terrorist organisation had claimed responsibility for the bomb, and it looked like Rachel was innocent of anything. The death toll from the hotel bomb was just under a dozen. That made it the worst terrorist act that Griffton had ever seen. Thirty-five people had been badly hurt. It was just horrible.

But what if Rachel was involved? It didn't bear thinking about. She did say she was going to take that strange package to a hotel. Or was it a restaurant? Lara's memory of their conversation was hazy because it had been so late at night. She didn't want to think about it anymore.

She took one last look at the magazines, her head awash with emotion, and walked reluctantly to the gate.

❧ 12345 ❧

IT HAD SEEMED like a long time since Rachel had dreamed about the mountains, but here in this little room with no windows, her mind gave her a panoramic view of the spiky, snow-capped peaks.

The long mountain range was so familiar now, as though she

had grown up on its slopes. It was somewhere in the east, near India or Nepal, she felt. She ran her hand over the dozen spiky summits, imagining herself to be a giant, towering over a tiny model.

She looked down at the hard ice which covered the sheer cliff faces. She had a bird's-eye view of the angular rocks, massive, sheer drops, and angel-white snow. She saw the grey and black rock peeking out from underneath the ice. There were the deep chasms and the sounds of the treacherous winds whipping at her ears.

Then she saw the double-peaked mountain with its hard edges. That mountain, which used to rumble in her dreams, was now roaring. Or was it the wind? No, it was definitely the mountain. It roared a full-throated roar. The mountain was roaring in pain.

Halfway up, she could see a fissure starting to tear open. First, she saw a thin black line being carved diagonally up the steep mountain. This turned into a crack and then something resembling a doorway. The roar came from this opening.

It called to her.

Rocks tumbled hundreds of feet down to crash at the base of the mountain. Rachel had a sense of foreboding and felt utterly wretched and helpless. She was no longer a giant overshadowing the mountain but a tiny figure at its foot. The mountain towered over her, and the other world beckoned her through the portal. She knew the giants lived there, through the doorway. The Nephilim.

"They're coming," she murmured to herself in the dream. "They're coming," she smiled, looking towards the doorway between worlds. Her eyes were glowing again as she slept. In her dream, something terrified her: something about herself. It was the evil inside her own heart.

Rachel screamed herself awake.

LAKE HEARD the scream and sat bolt upright on the top of his crates. He had been lying across four crates, lined up in a row by one of the walls. Moonlight illuminated the storeroom through the barred windows.

"Rachel?" he shouted. "Rachel, is that you?"

Rachel had been on his mind constantly. He could see her big brown eyes wherever he looked. Somehow, the thought he might see her again was helping to get him through his ordeal here.

She had already come to the house once, though he hadn't managed to attract her attention that time. He had tried to float that card aeroplane out of the window. The one made from a nightclub flyer. But the plan hadn't worked. After that, he didn't know whether she was alive or dead. But he doggedly held onto the hope that the men had spared her life.

Now that he was confident she was alive, his hope rose again. He was convinced he had heard her voice and wasn't imagining things. It seemed to come from somewhere beneath him. Perhaps from a subterranean basement room. She sounded like she was in trouble and needed rescuing. That made two of them.

He leapt off his box, scrambled across the room, and tried the door for the thousandth time. He pushed and pulled it in vain. No joy. He tried hammering on it and shouting. But this also had no effect.

"Some hero I am," he complained to himself. He stood panting, his hands on his thighs.

RACHEL SNAPPED out of her dream. She sat shaking on her bed, adrenaline flowing through her body from the scream. She panted lightly and stared around her, half expecting a monster to leap out of the darkness of the corners of her room.

She sat on her blanket in the darkness of the small windowless room and looked around. It was cold, but she didn't know whether it was day or night. A small glow reached in from under her door. It enabled her to make out the edge of the table and chair but little else.

Memories of the mountains and the portal clouded her mind. She turned to look into the darkness.

The next second, her door cracked off its hinges and spun outwards. It sent bright light into her room from the hall. The door flew back and cracked against the wall opposite. It fractured with the force of the blow, then slumped onto the floor in pieces.

A figure walked calmly into the room. A muscular man in his middle years with short-cropped hair.

"You must be Rachel Race," boomed the man with a smile. His voice was deep and humorous. "At last, we get to meet," he added.

He offered her a strong hand and virtually pulled her off the bed as he shook it. Rachel stared at him, stunned. Deep down, she knew she was safe at last.

Then it occurred to her that she had seen this man before. It hadn't been in the flesh like this, but perhaps in one of her strange visions. Was he the man from the mountains who had fought the panther for her?

"Sorry, I'm forgetting my manners. Caleb Noble," he beamed as though it explained everything.

"Erm, Rachel Race," mumbled Rachel. "But, like, I guess you already knew that, right?"

"It's good to finally meet you, Rachel Race," rejoiced Caleb kindly. "What you did back there in the hotel was the right thing to do. The Dunamis told me everything."

"But it didn't make any difference," Rachel agonised. "They still…"

"It's okay. You are not responsible," consoled Caleb. "You showed what was in your heart. You were willing to sacrifice yourself when it came down to it to save those people. You did good, Rachel."

Then he suddenly added, "Are you coming?"

"What? Now?" she asked.

Caleb led her out of her prison and onto the stone floor of the corridor. Rachel realised she didn't have any shoes on.

"Er, my shoes…" she said, but Caleb had already produced them in one hand and was giving them to her.

"Thanks," she smiled.

Then she noticed the bodies lying on the floor further up.

"Are they dead?" she stammered, her big eyes growing bigger as she regarded them.

"No, not dead. Just senseless."

"Senseless?"

"Senseless as in 'senseless violence.' It was meant to be a joke," shrugged Caleb.

"Oh," said Rachel, and added, "Are they going to be, like, all right?"

"The Dunamis is working on them. He's doing business at the moment. After that, yes, they will be better than before."

"Who exactly are you?"

"I'm no one special. But wait until you meet the Dunamis. He's the one worth knowing," smiled Caleb.

"Dunamis?"

"Yeah."

"Could you, like, go a bit slower with everything? I'm kind of getting freaked out here," asked Rachel honestly. "Have you seen Lake?"

"A lake?"

"Lake Emerson – he's a guy. He's, like, my friend, and he's here somewhere. We need to get him. They've got him locked up. Like me."

"I'll ask the Dunamis," said Caleb. They approached a flight of grey stone steps which led upwards.

"Okay, this way," said Caleb.

At the top of the stairs, they came to a dark hallway with

three exits. Bare light bulbs were visible in the moonlight that fell from a long window on the far side. Caleb led the way across the hallway and down a long corridor.

It ran along the length of the house and had several doors in it. The furthest door opened, and two men burst out.

Rachel recognised one of them as being the older, tanned man with a lined face. He was scowling, his face distorted with rage. The two men started to rush towards them. Caleb pushed Rachel behind him with one arm. He held up his other palm in front of him and closed his eyes.

CHAPTER 25

Reflected in Rachel's big brown irises was the flash of light that seemed to come from Caleb Noble's palm. She saw the two assailants physically thrown across the corridor and land on their backs, where they lay stock still.

"Remember to breathe," Caleb told her.

Rachel let out the huge breath which she had stored up.

"Young girl, the power of the Dunamis is greater than any obstacle," said Caleb.

Rachel nodded, her eyes still wide open. She pushed her hair out of her face.

"He's in here," said Caleb. He marched up to the door at the end. Then, rather undramatically, he slid the lock across and opened the door normally.

Lake Emerson let out an aggressive holler and charged at Caleb with his head down.

Caleb, a clear foot taller than the young man, somehow managed to restrain Lake by putting his hand on his shoulder. "It's okay," he laughed. "It's okay, Lake. It's over now."

But Lake was panting, with tears welling up in his eyes. He had been trying to be brave for so long and save his energy for the moment when he could jump another of his captors.

Then, when he saw Rachel, cute little big-eyed Rachel, standing there in the corridor behind the strong man, Lake couldn't hold back the tears. The reality of his freedom was overwhelming. He wished she could have seen him being strong, as he had been all this time. But instead, she had to see him like this.

Rachel ran forward and threw her arms around his neck. He wept into her shoulder.

"I was coming to rescue you," whispered Lake in a disjointed manner. "I was," he added.

She shushed him, and they melted into the moment.

"OH MY GOODNESS," cried Rachel. "That means you were, like, right about the Nephilim and the mountain and all that stuff you sent me. And I thought you were playing a massive practical joke on me – what an idiot I am," said Rachel.

Lake said nothing. He sat there in the front room of the house with his mind-boggling. He was still getting used to the idea that he was free. And that there were men lying strewn across the house. But that this was somehow "all right," according to this strange warrior dude who'd turned up and laid them all out without so much as touching them.

But he was glad they had found the kitchens and a good supply of food, which they were munching through. They had all sorts of cakes and biscuits and fizzy drinks, and Caleb even found some frozen pizzas, which they cooked up in the oven. It made a change from all the gruel they had been feeding him, thought Lake.

"Now, why couldn't they have given me any of this stuff?" he joked.

He really wanted to phone his parents to tell them he was all right, but Caleb assured him there would be time for that. It was three thirty in the morning anyway.

"So, just to recap," said Rachel. "Those mountains I've been dreaming about are in Nepal. And the big one is called Makalu, right? There's some sort of doorway between worlds, some sort of portal, in the mountains, and you've been there?"

Caleb nodded.

"So Samyaza and the Nephilim are somewhere in there, and they're trying to break out and come back into the world, which would be, like, a really bad thing, yes?"

"How can this Samyaza be bound up under a mountain and running around here at the same time?" Lake blurted out.

"Good question, Master Emerson," noted Caleb.

"You like that question? I've got more. Like a hundred more," jabbered Lake.

"At the moment, Samyaza can only have an indirect influence on the earth by using individuals who choose to follow him. But when the portal opens, he will be freed."

"Oh great," lamented Lake.

"And what about this portal thing? How does it get opened?"

"We don't know," said Caleb.

"Okay, fine. I've got plenty more questions. Are you ready? Here they are. First of all, 'Who are you?' Next is: 'Why are you here?' Then, 'How did you know to come here? How did you do all that stuff? And what are we going to do?'" ranted Lake.

"Very good questions. Me? I'm a slave of the one who creates and sustains. I'm a slave to the light. A slave and a friend. Some people choose to be slaves to the darkness, like these men, and that's their choice. But my master is good. It's his nature to love us. Would you like to meet the Dunamis? It will help you understand."

"The who?" asked Lake.

"My master sent him to give us power," Caleb said in the way of explanation.

"I don't know," said Lake.

"It'll answer a lot of your questions, believe me. He is the one who has the plan and the power and knows what we need to do," explained Caleb.

"I'd like to meet him," said Rachel. She stared at Lake, eyes wide open.

Lake cautiously agreed, so Caleb closed his eyes for a moment and called on the Dunamis to fill the place.

Then, very quickly, something like a river started to flow through the front room. But rather than being made of water, it was a river of pure spirit, and it was good. They could all see the river, but not with their eyes. Lake and Rachel were stunned by the powerful encounter with this new force, which left them reeling.

"It's okay to breathe," informed Caleb, as his new friends felt the river flow through their bodies and renew their tired limbs.

Rachel went under the waters of the river and enjoyed the sensation. It warmed her senses and her spirit. Amazingly, she could no longer feel the throb in her hand at the stump of her severed finger. The pain from Lake's bruised ribs also disappeared, and he started to feel drunk. They found themselves giggling.

"This Dunamis is Dynamite!" Lake laughed. He was already trying to decide how he might describe the experience in words. It was kind of electric, kind of like drowning, but more like living. Blading really fast down a hill was what it was like! Maybe it was like jumping into a bath filled with warm water, which also contained a toaster that was plugged into the mains.

Above all, he had the feeling of overwhelming love and power. "I'm just going to lie here on the floor for a bit, if that's, like, okay with you guys," Rachel sang out. She was awash with the power of the Dunamis and was feeling incredibly carefree. As another wave of the spirit river hit her, she crumpled on the floor. She just managed to hear Caleb saying something before she fell into a deep sleep.

"Be refreshed. Then, return home in the morning, both of you. We'll meet again, I'm sure," he said.

"When?" murmured Lake before he, too, collapsed onto the floor, mightily relaxed.

"I don't know. I have my path to travel, and you have yours. But we will meet again. The Dunamis protect you," said Caleb.

Then he slipped out of the door.

12345

MEANWHILE, Rachel's father, Eddie, was sobbing into another glass of whisky. He had worked all day, a carpentry job at a business park on lower west Griffton. His hands were calloused and tired from working with wood. After that, he had drunk whisky all evening and hadn't showered. He stank.

Work had been hard to come by over recent years. So, he made the decision to be flexible and diversify the jobs he offered customers. He loved working with his hands and was good at it. Plumbers and carpenters could command a good rate down in the South, and the work gave him a sense of satisfaction that he could at least get something right in his life. It was a far cry from teaching, the career he had a lifetime ago. But then, the naïve English teacher from Birmingham - who had met the beautiful Maryam in Kerala all those years ago - that man was long gone.

Everything had changed after his wife died. Where his love used to be grew a newfound hate. Instead of joy, he had dissatisfaction. Replacing his peace was a daily strife that gnawed at his insides. He was impatient, unkind, and low in self-control.

Now he had to face all this again: visitations from an old 'friend,' or should that be 'fiend'?

"I did what you asked me to do," he said, red-eyed. "You promised you would leave me alone after that if I did that one last thing for you," he cried, his Midlands accent slipping back.

"Promises, promises," sneered Samyaza. "You should know by now that I am just not able to keep my promises. You just can't trust me."

"You're codding me," said Eddie.

Eddie was sitting in an empty house on the sofa, which bore the indentation of his bottom because he sat there so often. Tonight, his house had become a prison, and this evil fiend was his jailer.

"My own little baby. What have I done?" he cried. "You made me cut off her finger. You forced me to do it. But I don't remember. Was it me? You devil."

"Flattery will get you everywhere," joked Samyaza. "Listen, everyone makes choices. Remember, you came looking for me. All that time ago."

"Now I've lost her for good," continued Eddie. "If you tell her it was me, she'll run and never come back. Or they'll take her. You can't tell her it was me. She'll kill me. Or worse."

"Calm down, there, Eddie. I'm not going to do anything as long as you keep quiet. I need you on standby, that's all. Ready for action."

He called Samyaza all the names he could think of and then doubled over, bowing down to the floor to pour himself another glass of whisky. He stayed silent as he carried out the action, then thoughtfully screwed the cap on the bottle.

"Okay. Just don't hurt her, that's all. She's all I've got," he pleaded.

CHAPTER 26

Lake Emerson had the story of a lifetime, one that catapulted him from being the junior researcher at the Griffton News to a fully-fledged reporter. It was a crackerjack story. A member of the Griffton News team had been snatched in his own home and taken against his will by a gang of subversive occultists, kept for dark reasons, and eventually rescued by a publicity-shy Good Samaritan.

Even better was the fact that the captive could tell his own story. Everything was authentic: the sights, the smells, and the emotions. This also meant his mum could get to see her eighteen-year-old son's name in print at last.

Anne made sure the editorial assistant Kimberley lost her job for her lies, telling her Lake had gone away on assignment to Polcombe, the cheek of the girl. After a brief investigation, where Kimberley gave no good reason for her behaviour, the Griffton News editor shook his head and showed her the door. Then, life on the paper carried on as normal, publishing being no stranger to hiring and firing.

Lake was purposefully fuzzy on some of the details of his escape, such as how he and Rachel had escaped their prisons. The truth was too insane. What he did say was that a reluctant hero from out of town had heard their cries as he passed by. It wasn't entirely true. But he said the stranger had rescued them and gone on his way, and that was true. He also made sure to mention the rats and the disgusting gruel they fed him.

When the story of his capture came out, it was splashed across the front cover of the newspaper. It had Lake's picture and a special feature on how he had survived the ordeal by keeping hold of hope and thinking about seeing his new girlfriend, Rachel Race, also pictured. Lake went on local radio and found a small amount of celebrity, which helped him to make his name as a writer. Rachel was proud of him.

The occultists were all captured, except for the one young man who had carried out the hotel bombing and, sadly, hadn't survived the explosion. The occultists admitted to the whole thing, and the police found evidence both of preparations for the attack and the materials themselves and prosecuted them as terrorists. They were, in due course, charged and locked up.

No one mentioned Rachel's part in the bomb plot, and she decided to keep quiet rather than end up being arrested. It was a tough decision and not one she took lightly. But all she wanted to do was go home and try to rebuild her life, such as it was.

❦ 12345 ❦

DANIEL REAPPEARED BACK at his house one morning, explaining to his family that he had suddenly been called away on business, which was, in fact, not an unusual situation for the Harcourt family.

Arabella put her arms around him on the porch, glad to have him back. She decided not to ask him right away about the note he had left on the bedside table or the watch and rings he had left for the boys.

His note had simply said: *My dearest Arabella, I have to leave immediately to attend to business abroad and may be some time. I will contact you soon, but know that I love you very much. Daniel.*

She decided not to ask him about it all just yet because she noticed something very different about him. It was his eyes. They were softer, clearer, and brighter. And he had a fresh lightness about him. In fact, she felt as though she had a completely new husband but couldn't put her finger on what else had changed. She trusted that Daniel would tell her what he needed to when the time was right.

After he had hugged his boys and had a coffee with his wife, he headed to his study to work, as he had a lot of work to do, so he told them. What he hadn't chosen to tell her was that he had determined to make amends to all the people he had wronged through the years of doing Samyaza's bidding. The ones he could, anyway.

This included, more recently, the pharmacist at Lupus Street Chemist, whom he had knocked out with chloroform and stolen various chemical ingredients so the Samyaza followers could make their bomb. He sent money anonymously, a large amount of it, and an apology, and that would have to be a start. He didn't fancy going to the police and confessing all just yet but was prepared to do so if he must.

After that, he started working backwards, set on doing whatever he had to in order to make amends. After all, he was a slave to the light now, and he knew the Dunamis would be on his case until he did the right thing.

"We're all slaves to something," Caleb Noble had told him. "For some, it's a slave to self; for others, it's your addictions or possessions. For others, it's money or power. For you, it was Samyaza. Me, I'm a slave to the Dunamis, and do you know what? Every day's an adventure."

LAKE AND RACHEL sat hand in hand up on Griffton Cliff, watching another sunset over the sea. The skies were clear, which meant another cool night, and Lake and Rachel were happy and in love. They gazed at the tops of the buildings. A lot happened in a short time in a small area: this wonderful seaside city of Griffton. The trials had aged them a little, though they had not made them jaded.

Looking down, the memories sprang forth again, vibrant and present. There was Griffton General Hospital, where they had patched up Rachel's hand, and she had almost been gored by a panther. Griffton Library was at the centre where Rachel had been grabbed by the vagrant and met Lake in the basement, and there was the Griffton News tower near the central mall. Over there was the wreckage of the Griffton Metropolitan Hotel, where the psychopaths had detonated their bomb.

All the little flats and houses lay beneath them in the valley, and Ramshack Café and Rock and Shock were somewhere down there at the seafront, where surfers and skaters filled the wonderful Griffton beaches, frolicking and laughing under the evening sun. The summer was in full bloom.

"Do you reckon we'll see Caleb Noble soon?" Rachel asked.

"Do you reckon we'll see him at all?" asked Lake.

"Oh, I think so. We've got to stop the end of the world, remember?"

"Yeah, I guess so. Hey, knock, knock."

"Oh no: not another knock, knock joke. Who's there?" said Rachel reluctantly.

"Armageddon!"

"Armageddon, who?"

"Armageddon out of here!"

"Oh, Lake, that is so old," she complained.

"Okay, then try this: an old snake goes to see his doctor. 'Doctor, I need something for my eyes… I can't see so well these days,' he says. The doctor fixes him up with a pair of glasses and tells him to return in a fortnight. So, the snake comes back in two weeks and tells the doctor he's very depressed. The doc says, 'What's the problem? Didn't the glasses help you at all?' The snake replies, 'The glasses are fine, doctor, I just discovered I've been living with a water hose the past two years!'"

Rachel giggled. "You're funny."

Then, she added rather randomly, "My dad hasn't been himself lately. I mean, he has been himself, which is never great, but he's just so, like, distant. It's like everything's changed. I mean, Lara going away, and everything else. She's still not replying to my messages," lamented Rachel.

"Yeah? Well, you've still got Rock and Shock and Iona," said Lake. "And you've got me," he added shyly.

Rachel looked into his eyes for a moment and smiled.

Lake was right. Things weren't so bad after all, she thought. Her seventeenth birthday was under a year away, which meant she could get a car. Rock and Shock was still great fun. She was about to start a couple of days of filing and phone work in a publisher's office near Lake's work. They could meet for lunch. And it would be good to have more money coming in and make some new friends.

"Tell me another one of your jokes, then," she said. Lake beamed.

BOLIVIA, Central South America.

José Antonio lay in bed after a hot day of farming soybeans on his father's farm. He shared a bedroom with Carlos, Diego, and Sergio, his brothers, who also worked alongside him on the land. He had walked for miles today under the merciless sun and was glad to finally get to his bed. His sisters, Evita and Luisa, had gone to bed sometime before the boys, who wanted to fool and tumble around, tired though they all were.

As he drifted into a powerful sleep that dragged him quickly beneath the surface, he started to dream that dream again. It was the one about the mountains.

He had travelled to the Andes Mountains several times and seen the Bolivian Altiplano in the west, his country's section of the Andes. But these mountains in his dreams seemed different. They were harder and bigger, and the snow blew all the time.

In his mind, he saw the snow and black ice wedged against the steep cliff faces of the mountain. Then he saw a long tear in the mountain, like someone had taken some cloth with both hands and pulled it apart. It was like the mountain was cracking open. It was just like the other year when he had fallen out of a tree onto a rock and cut his leg open. He watched the rip in the mountain grow until it was a doorway that seemed to lead into the very heart of the mountains. Then he saw something else. It was a whirlwind of snow and ice, and it came right out of the doorway.

The powerful spinning vortex lifted away from the doorway and sat outside it, rotating in the air, growing taller by the second.

Suddenly, José Antonio felt a sharp pain in his left hand and let out a cry. He thought the dog had bitten him, and he angrily sat up in his bed to scold him. But he couldn't see the family dog anywhere.

Then he noticed in the half-light that he was bleeding from his left hand. He quickly placed his right hand over the cut and realised his finger was missing.

It was his fourth: the one between his little finger and his middle one.

He cried out again in pain, watching with tears in his eyes as his brothers jumped up in their beds.

Before long, the entire household was awake.

ACKNOWLEDGMENTS

The author would like to thank R, J and C for their love and kindness, Dora Taylor for her friendship and support; Louis for his creativity; Pete Champneys, my friends at The Book Whisperer, and the wonderful people at JAC Design.

About the Author

Joshua Raven has enjoyed thirty years as an international journalist, editor, business copywriter and media consultant. As a novelist he has been a featured author at the Dubai Emirates Airline Festival of Literature. And as a journalist and professional writer he has interviewed leading figures in business and technology, including Bill Gates and Michael Dell, and written for publications and businesses across the globe including The Times newspaper, Microsoft, Google and Facebook. Joshua lives in the South of England and enjoys people, music, cooking, reading, and travelling.

facebook.com/JoshuaRavenAuthor

x.com/RavenWrites

instagram.com/RavenWrites

linkedin.com/in/arif-mohamed-71b2831a

amazon.com/stores/Joshua-Raven/author/B0034O22RS

pinterest.com/joshuaraven75

ALSO BY JOSHUA RAVEN